Once And For All

By

Amy Durham

ISBN: 978-0-9850706-4-9

DEDICATION

To my boys… the remarkable musician, the budding artist, and the future drummer… may you find your places in this world and never sacrifice one bit of yourselves in the process. You are enough, exactly as you are.

ACKNOWLEDGMENTS

As always, I send out a very heartfelt thanks to the community of writers I am fortunate to be a part of: the wonderful members of Kentucky Romance Writers, who have been a source of encouragement for many years, the fantastic authors in the Kentucky Independent Writers network who are a wealth of both information and inspiration, and Ray Hollenbach and the local writers in my hometown who provide an avenue for sharing the creative side of myself.

Kari Lee Townsend, thank you once again for your insightful and honest critiquing which has made this book better and stronger. Teresa Reasor and J.M. Madden, thank you for always being willing to read and give feedback. I don't know what I'd do without you girls!

I cannot say enough thanks to my amazing family. My husband Kevin, and my beautiful boys, Kelly, Eli, and Reece, fill my life with love and laughter, and more joy than I could've ever imagined. Thanks also to my parents, who not only gave me a foundation for my life, but also continue to be pillars of support and wisdom.

To my friend, Cayce Davenport, the real-life Miss Stockton, thank you for friendship, laughter, and teaching me a bit about sculpture and carving tools!

And thank you readers! Without you, all of this would be for naught!

PROLOGUE

How nice that at least one person was not in the *Phoebe-Campbell-is-a-freak* club.

I liked Mr. Pierce, the guy who owned the hardware store. Apparently he was too old to realize I was the most uncool person in Sky Cove.

I crunched across the snowy mush in the hardware store parking lot. Typical Maine, the day before New Year's Eve was drab, gray, and bitter cold, but I didn't care.

I needed paint. And wood. And other artsy stuff.

I loved Christmas break. Not because I got all crazy with holiday spirit, but because it meant a break from the black hole known as Sky Cove Senior High School. It also meant loads of time spent in the little spare bedroom that my dad had let me turn into an art studio two years ago.

Head down, I did my best to shield myself against the biting wind, pushing toward the front door of Pierce Home Improvement. Winter in Maine always sucked, but the icy wind made today worse than usual. I was almost there, just about to step inside and out of the icebox, when the door opened and someone in a really nice pair of leather boots pounded out.

And straight into me.

My center of gravity already off from walking half bent over with my head lowered out of the wind, I lost my balance and tumbled back.

Right onto my butt.

And even through several layers of clothes and a heavy coat, the ground was wet and cold against my backside.

Great.

But it got worse.

Staring down at me was the dumb jock football star, at whose feet all of Sky Cove Senior High worshipped.

Todd Miller, with his designer jeans and expensive black coat.

"Uh, Sorry," he said, his eyes locked uncomfortably on mine, but not bothering to help me up.

Like I needed his help.

Making matters worse was the fact that he was so freaking cute. And yeah, I'd noticed that a long time ago. Unfortunately, every time he opened his mouth all the cuteness went away.

I pushed up, gaining my feet without slipping again on the ice. The stupid moron just stood there continuing to stare at me.

"Watch where you're going," I snapped, and walked inside, leaving him standing there in the cold.

Bad enough I had to deal with the idiots from Sky Cove Senior High during regular school hours. Running into them – literally – outside of school just put me in a bad mood.

Worse mood, I corrected.

Twenty minutes later, I emerged from the store, a large bag of paint, wood, and other supplies dangling from one arm. A glance toward the near-empty parking lot told that Todd Miller and his big, stupid truck were long gone.

Thank God for small favors.

At home, I went straight to my studio. The bedroom-turned-work-area was cluttered with art supplies, paper, in-progress artwork, and I loved every inch of it.

I'd developed an idea for a shadow-box display of small wooden carvings depicting Maine wildlife. Getting accepted to college wasn't the problem for me, but paying for it would be. I had high hopes that I could pick up some scholarship money in the Coastal Maine Artists Guild student art competition.

Inspiration came quickly and pretty soon my hands took over, each subtractive action of my carving knife and V-tool bringing the figure further to life. The grain of the scrap maple hardwood Mr. Pierce had given me gave extra dimension to the little animal taking shape in my hands.

I wasn't sure how long I worked, but when I finished, I sat the small red fox on the table and leaned back to look.

And smiled.

It was so life like, so playful. As if I'd somehow captured its personality.

If I could create more like this, maybe a bear and a moose, the display would be spectacular.

My gaze narrowed, and my peripheral vision seemed to fall away, leaving only a small tunnel of sight that was trained on the small fox figurine. I wanted to blink, to shake my head and make my eyesight return to normal, but I could not take my eyes off the fox.

Then I wasn't looking at the figure anymore. In front of my eyes I saw what could only be the floor of a forest. Snow covered the ground, dotted with fallen leaves and twigs. Tree branches moved and creaked with the wind.

The forest was dark, as if I were seeing it exactly the way it would look at this precise moment, and all around me I heard the organic silence of the woods.

My heartbeat picked up and my breathing became rapid as fear surged through me. Fear of what I had no clue - the scene in front of me was benign enough – but I felt it nonetheless.

Lost. I felt lost. Completely enveloped in the unknown. Suffocated by the lack of reality.

What in the world was happening?

The sight of the forest was not unfamiliar, but somehow it felt totally foreign to me and I wanted desperately to escape.

The front door opened, and I heard my dad call my name. I blinked away the fog.

And I was looking at my tiny red fox again.

Crazy.

CHAPTER 1

One more semester. Four and a half months. Eighteen weeks. It seemed like forever.

But I could make it. Because then I'd be done with this place, and all the people in it, forever.

Graduation was a bright, welcoming light looming at the end of a long, dark tunnel.

I defied the dress code and pulled my hood up over the ponytail that held my long blond hair, plowing my way through the crowded hallways of Sky Cove Senior High. Long ago I'd ceased to notice the aging appearance of the building – discolored ceiling tiles, cracks in the concrete block walls, door facings with little to no finish left on them – but today, as I started my last semester of school in this wretched place, I took note. I wanted to look at this place that had given me nothing but crap, so that when I was finally gone for good I'd be even more thrilled.

I dodged cliques of students loitering around their lockers or the water fountains. I'd never admit it - and it made me nauseous to know it was true - but I actually sort of envied them.

What would it be like to always have people to talk to?

Snap out of it, Phoebe! I ordered myself to lose the self-pitying thoughts. It was ridiculous to be jealous of kids whose entire existence centered around clothes, shoes, and dating.

Superficial fools.

I'd suffered their ridicule and ignorance for the past eight years, since moving to Sky Cove with my father at the age of nine. I'd jump off a cliff before I wished to be like any of them.

After enduring senior English, American government, pre-calculus, advanced biology, and sociology – not to mention the always-pleasant cafeteria lunch – I was looking forward to my last class of the day.

Advanced art.

Where I could finally escape and be myself.

And enjoy something. For at least part of the school day.

For the past four years, I'd spent my electives taking every art class Sky Cove offered, which, unfortunately, was not a lot. But it was enough to fuel my creativity. I was good at it, and it was the one place I didn't feel quite so excluded. Maybe I wasn't best buddies with the other kids in the class, but I did have a few friends, and the others weren't so high up the social ladder that they looked down their noses at me.

At least I could breathe in their presence.

Then I walked in the room.

And among the familiar faces and expected classmates was an anomaly. An error. Stupidity personified.

Todd Miller.

Tall, broad, and so completely out of place in the art classroom. Wearing his Sky Cove Senior High football sweatshirt with his name and number adorning the back.

My sanctuary had been tainted.

The warning bell sounded its dull, warped ring, and I took my seat. If there was a consolation to be found in this crazy situation, it was that the art geeks talked among themselves and no one seemed to be paying any attention to Todd Miller.

I wondered how he liked that feeling.

Under normal circumstances my art teacher, Miss Stockton, thirty-something, spunky, and always dressed in that cute, funky way of artists, made high school somewhat bearable. She'd returned to Sky Cove, the town where she grew up, three years ago, and taken the art class reigns from the very dry and anti-fun Mrs. Howard, who retired after like sixty years of teaching. It was only natural that I'd love Miss Stockton. She did, after all, teach the one subject I cared about. And she did, in fact, offer the only place in the building where I felt something close to normalness.

Today was not normal.

Todd Miller's presence loomed like a heavy, gray cloud.

And our assignment for the foreseeable future dropped like a bomb.

"Our class is going to present an art show," Miss Stockton said. "Just like a gallery opening, with guests, refreshments, tasteful displays. You're each welcome to submit some of your individual pieces for the show."

This part was exciting. The next part totally sucked.

"You're also going to work in pairs to create larger projects. We want to demonstrate cooperation and collective creativity."

Pairs? Are you kidding me? I didn't like anybody else. And I sure as heck didn't trust anyone else to have a hand in my artwork. I worked alone. Period.

"There are eighteen of you, which means nine large projects," she went on. "And we're going to draw names to determine partners. The more experienced art students will each be paired with a less experienced one."

Draw names? Could this possibly get any worse?

I shouldn't have asked that. Because yes, it absolutely could get worse.

Miss Stockton walked to my table first, holding a bowl with slips of paper that presumably had the names of the novices on them.

She held the bowl out to me. I stared at it with hatred, as

if the moment my hand reached in I would be infected with a nasty, flesh-eating bacteria.

With no other choice, I took a slip of paper, and was overwhelmed with a ridiculous feeling that something irrevocable and life-changing had just happened.

I don't know why I even bothered to look. But when I did, I was not surprised.

Todd Miller.

I resisted, barely, the urge to slide low in my seat and pull my hoodie over my head and halfway down my face. Besides being against the stupid dress code, Miss Stockton always told me I wasn't allowed to hide in her classroom.

After a bit of discussion about our class syllabus, the bell rang, ending the period and the school day, and kids sprinted for the door.

I walked up to Miss Stockton's desk, sure that I could do something remedy this situation.

"I need a different partner." I told myself that if I stated it rather than asking, it would go my way. Might've helped if my voice had sounded like an adult, rather than a squeaky mouse. I stood straight, maintaining eye contact, and hoped I appeared more adult than my huge gray sweatshirt and baggy carpenter jeans looked.

Miss Stockton just looked at me with her eyebrows raised, blonde bangs falling across one eye. "Why?"

I dropped the slip of paper with Miller's name on it in front of her. In my mind, that explained it all.

"Phoebe, someone's got to work with him." Her voice was firm, yet soft with compassion. Which pretty much summed Miss Stockton up.

"Come on, Miss Stockton," I said, lowering my voice so I wouldn't be heard by any students loitering outside the door. "He's only in this class because he thinks it'll be an easy A."

"You don't know that," she said, peeking at me over the top rim of her glasses with an expression that made me wonder if she knew something she wasn't letting on.

"Have you ever known of Todd Miller to take anything

besides football and his social status seriously? He always takes the easy way out."

"Then it sounds like he has a lot to learn, and you, my brightest student, have a lot to teach him." She looked me straight in the eyes, and added, "And not just about art."

She pushed her glasses back into place and twirled the red pendant that hung from a long silver chain, turning to look at her computer screen.

End of discussion.

I wanted to pout. To stomp out and huff and puff and roll my eyes at this lunacy. But, Miss Stockton's opinion of me was too important to jeopardize.

So instead, I walked out of the room quietly, and with as much dignity as I could manage. I tried to imagine all the ways this assignment would suck, but there were too many to count.

However, there was always the hope that Miller would just let me do all the work. Then I wouldn't actually have to work with him. I considered this as I made my way toward the front door, my steps echoing in the emptying hallway. I could just show him the project at various intervals so he'd be able to act like he knew what was going on.

I mean, surely he didn't really want to work, right?

I turned the corner into the lobby to head for the door, thinking that this might not turn out so bad after all.

It was an illusion that lasted all of two seconds, as I was confronted with his tall frame the minute I stepped into the tiny lobby.

"So I guess we're partners, huh?"

CHAPTER 2

Had he really waited for me?

It seemed so crazy.

Almost as crazy as the fact that his voice sounded deep and sincere and really, really nice.

And it was absolutely insane that I was noticing that right at this moment.

"Looks like," I answered.

He just stood there, silent, hands in the pockets of his blue jeans, looking at me. Dark brown hair cut short, but curling up slightly at the ends, blue eyes looking straight at me. His jaw tensed, as if he wanted to say something, but still he said nothing.

Forget the brown hair and blue eyes. I decided to take control of the situation. After all, the only way I was ever going to survive this stupid partnership was if I figured out a way to be completely in charge.

"Look, I know the score, okay?" I began. "I know you expect me to do all the work and be brilliant and then just put your name on it so you get half the credit."

He pushed away from the doorjamb he'd been leaning on and took a step toward me. "It's not that," he started to say, but I cut him off.

"And I'm okay with that," I said.

He looked at me like I'd grown a second head.

"I'm absolutely fine with that scenario," I reiterated.

His gaze blinked away from me, and for a split second I almost thought I saw an expression of hurt cross his face.

Almost.

Because there was no way Todd Miller was going to be hurt by anything I said.

"I don't expect you to do all the work." His voice was quiet, with a touch of humility.

Was I losing my freaking mind?

He continued. "I mean, I know I can't help with a lot of it, because you're the expert and everything, but I can run errands, get supplies, clean up, that sort of thing."

A group of kids from the Ag shop rounded the corner, heavy boots thundering against the tile floor. The FFA guys didn't exactly run in the same circles as Miller, but they knew enough to look twice when they saw the two of us having a conversation.

"Grunt work?" I asked. "You really want to do grunt work?"

"I want to help however I can."

I glanced around. The secretary in the front office was busy staring at her computer screen. Cars streamed out of the parking lot. No sound came from the hallway.

I took a step closer to him, trying my best to seem intimidating, even though I didn't feel that way. Instead, stepping closer to him made me notice that my eyes were level with his chin, which had a very attractive cleft, and that whatever shampoo or cologne he used was warm and woodsy.

Yes, I was definitely losing my mind.

"What's with this accommodating attitude, Miller?" I put on my best don't-screw-with-me voice. It lacked the oomph I'd hoped for, but I went with it nonetheless. "Last I remembered, I wasn't even a speck of dust on your radar, and Mr. Popularity wouldn't be caught dead talking to the freaky art girl in the baggy clothes."

His eyes narrowed. He looked offended. Good. Lord knew he'd done his share of offending over the years.

"I just want to pull my weight," he said, going on the defensive. "The project's for a grade."

"And we wouldn't want this stupid art class to blow your sparkling 2.0 GPA."

It wasn't often I got the chance to really speak my mind to the Sky Cove elite, but when it happened, I usually enjoyed it.

Strange that I wasn't loving this snarky exchange.

Todd's eyes went to the cell phone clutched in my left hand. Before I even had a chance to wonder what his next move would be, he'd grabbed the phone from my hand.

"Hey!" I reached for the phone, but he stepped back.

"Think whatever you want," he said, punching keys on my phone. "But I want to be a part of this project in whatever way I can. Even if it's grunt work."

He held the phone toward me. I stared at it as if it was a foreign object. When I didn't immediately move to take it from him, he picked up my left hand and wrapped it around my cell.

"That's my number," he said. "And you can find me on Facebook. I'm sure we'll need to buy some supplies, so you can text me a list and I'll pick them up. You can make all the decisions and be the boss."

I stood there, stunned into silence. With his own words he'd given me exactly what I wanted. I was completely in charge of the project. Yet somehow, with his acquiescence, I felt less in control than before.

I should respond. Come back at him with some biting comment. Unfortunately, I couldn't think past the pounding of my pulse.

He took a step closer, and I felt heat flush my face.

Insanity was a definite possibility.

"And I'm sorry I knocked you down at Pierce's the other

day," he whispered.

He walked out of school, while I stood, still frozen in place, a crazy swirl of confusion barreling through me.

Was his voice really that nice?

Did he really smell that good?

Had he really just programmed his number into my phone?

And why in the world had I just let him have the last word?

CHAPTER 3

Carving was my thing, so for the project I decided on a high-relief sculpture, done in various pieces of wood mounted on a large flat surface, depicting the Sky Cove Harbor they way it would've looked in the early twentieth century. Not that Miller would have any idea what that meant. I figured I'd just tell him we were doing a 3-D carving. Which might still require further explanation.

After texting my dad, as I did every afternoon, to let him know I was home, I found the perfect picture online. It had a rocky shoreline in the foreground, a few small sailboats in the water, and a hillside dotted with lean-to houses in the background. Imagining the detail I could put into carving the rocky shore and tiny boats, a smile spread across my face. There would be plenty of wood shavings for Miller to sweep up, plenty of scrap wood to get rid of.

Crap! It dawned on me then. If Miller was going to be on clean up duty, he'd have to be here, in my house, in my most special, important space.

My studio.

I tried to work up a feeling of disgust at the thought of Todd Miller puttering around my studio, but the feeling didn't come. I couldn't put a name to what I *did* feel. Morbid curiosity? A strange sense of anticipation?

Maybe the juxtaposition of Todd Miller, Sky Cove's favorite son, on clean-up duty had created some weird sense of justice.

I saved the picture of the harbor on my flash drive and made a mental plan to sit down tomorrow after school and sketch out the individual parts of the sculpture and lay them out in a sort of maquette of what the final product would look like. And also to make a list of materials I'd need and get that to Miller. I had a Facebook profile, for all the good it did me. I rarely used it. But I supposed if it meant I could communicate with Miller without having to actually talk to him, I could do it.

Deciding I'd thought about Miller enough, I grabbed my bag of carving tools from the table and another small piece of scrap maple. I'd rather create.

Rolling my chair across the hardwood floor to my worktable, I went to work.

It didn't take long for the small lynx to begin to emerge from the wood. Though the face of the animal looked similar to a cat, the longer body made it unique. I spent the most time carving the face, particularly the eyes, my grip on the v-tool firm and sure. With each action, I could feel the lynx's gaze on me, as if rather than just making it life-like, I was *giving* it life.

The eyes focused, even seemed to move as if glancing around, the expression at first blank, then confused and bewildered.

I cut my eyes left and right, looking for the source of the animal's confusion, only to discover I was *there* again, the edge of a wooded area, sparse sunlight filtering through the tree branches, seeing everything from what could only be the lynx's point of view.

It was crazy, and yet somehow I wasn't startled by it this time. As the lynx moved deeper into the trees, I felt its uneasiness, its fear. The emotions weren't mine. I didn't own them. I felt them as if they were being transferred to me from someone else.

The sounds of a door opening and voices calling didn't pull me out of the vision this time, because they were a *part* of the vision. I heard them through the lynx's ears, and felt alarm spread through the creature as we hurried further into the woods, leaves and snow crunching beneath our steps, and concealed ourselves behind a large tree trunk.

The darkness seemed to close in around us. Footsteps made their way nearer, and with every moment we cowered behind the tree my heart hammered violently in my chest.

I tried to reason with myself. So what if someone saw us? What would be so out of the ordinary about seeing a wild animal in the forest?

But there was nothing ordinary about it on my end. The sense of being in the scene but *not* being there wreaked havoc on the parameters of what was real in my world.

I could not believe this was happening again. This was more than craziness. What if I dropped into one of these fugue states at school? Or in front of my dad? While driving my car?

The fear of what might happen coursed through me with such force that I trembled. And trembling in fear was *not* something I regularly did.

The small wooden figure slipped from my hand as I shuddered in anticipation or alarm or uncertainty or whatever it was. Thankfully, the sound of the carved lynx hitting the hardwood floor of my studio snapped me back to reality.

A glance at the corner of my computer screen told me it was almost midnight. I'd heard my dad come in before I started carving. I should sleep, but how could I?

My heart raced and my forehead broke out in sweat. My hands were freaking shaking. The first time it had been easy enough to convince myself this was some sort of stress-induced hallucination, but a second time? How could I be in my studio one second and the next be in the middle of a forest?

A sliver of worry ran through me that maybe I was losing my mind, but surely I'd realize it if that was happening.

And yeah, I'm sure that's what all crazies thought right before they went over the edge, right?

The thought of going to bed and laying in the dark made my stomach heave. With no other real option for passing the time, I opened a browser and logged into my Facebook.

CHAPTER 4

Sitting at my desk with my laptop, I found his profile easy enough. Typical of a guy his age, nothing of a personal nature appeared. No favorite books or movies, however he did have the required sports listed as his interests. His last status update had been in November, as football playoffs approached.

I clicked to send a friend request, then went back to my own profile to make sure there was nothing I'd be embarrassed for him to see.

Of course there wasn't. The bulk of my friends list consisted of fellow art geeks that I'd met online, and a few of the kids who took art at school. My profile picture wasn't even me. Instead I'd opted for a picture of Mark Chagall's *Lovers with Flowers.*

The heater kicked on, but the air was chilly enough that I was glad for my sweats and fuzzy socks. Winter nights in Maine were nasty cold.

The red notification flag appeared, letting me know my friend request had been accepted, just as a chat box popped up. It was Miller.

Todd: *Still awake?*

Me: *Clearly.*
Todd: *Me too.*
Me: *Clearly.*

Wasn't this just a brilliant conversation? Again, I reminded myself that if I wanted this stupid project to be successful, I had to take the lead.

Me: *I've mapped out our project. Will get you a supply list tomorrow.*

Todd: *OK.*

Me: *You don't have to pay for it all. We can split the cost.*

Todd: *I can spring for it, but whatever.*

Me: *I should get some sleep.*

Not that I was going to fall into slumber any time soon after that freaky vision.

Todd: *Me too but I'm too pissed.*

Me: *Why?*

Todd: *My dad's all over me. He thinks I snuck out.*

Me: *Did you?*

Todd: *No. Well sort of. But just to the backyard.*

Me: *What for?*

Todd: *Nothing. It's stupid I gotta go.*

And then he was gone.

I didn't care why his dad was mad at him or whether he'd snuck into the back yard to smoke weed or meet some girl.

And yet, I was still wondering about it twenty minutes later, and hoping he hadn't gotten into much trouble -instead of sleeping.

***

Humidity hung in the air as swirls of mist, each breath I drew a burst of steam in my lungs. The forest around me was silent, save for the soft breeze that moved through the trees. I felt totally confused about what time or place I'd dropped into, yet feelings of alarm did not come. Instead, there was a peacefulness in this warm, summer forest.

I saw the outline of the woman, but not the features. Her

face was hidden by the shadows of the trees that surrounded her. The emerald green of her dress shimmered in the darkness and the soft yellow waves of her hair moved with the wind.

I didn't know her, and yet she was not a stranger.

"He must see you." Her voice listed toward me, as she spoke in a language I'd never heard, but somehow understood.

The words reached my ears, but I did not understand. Desperate for an explanation, I opened my mouth to speak, but no sound emerged.

As the scene around me began to fade, I heard her words again, singing through the breeze. "He must see you."

When I opened my eyes, I was in my bedroom, the pitch black outside my window telling me it was not yet morning. I shivered in the chill of the night air, a startling contrast to the warmth of my dream. While not frightening, the dream left me with an unsettling heaviness that found its way into my chest, and was still there when I finally drifted back to sleep.

CHAPTER 5

"School okay?" my dad asked over breakfast the next morning.

We had a nice routine going in our little house on Cliffhaven Lane. Dad worked second shift at the paper factory, so during the week, breakfast was our family time. We sat around our little four-seat dining table and caught up.

"Fine." I dug back into my bowl of Fruit Loops, still groggy from interrupted sleep. The bright yellow of the tablecloth annoyed me this morning. "Same."

I loved my dad. Charlie Campbell was as good as they came. He did his best for us after my mom died. He moved us out of the city to a town with a lower crime rate and more affordable cost of living. He couldn't be a mother to me, so he'd been the best father he could. Which was why I never talked to him about the miseries of Sky Cove Senior High. That was *not* fodder for breakfast conversation in our tiny kitchen.

I figured he knew I wasn't Ms. Popularity, but I let him believe it was my own choice, and in a way, it was. It would kill him to know how disliked I really was. My status at school didn't matter anyway. In a few short months it would all be over.

"Miss Stockton assigned a big art project," I said.

"Excited?" Dad asked.

"Not really. We have to work in pairs."

"Might be good for you. You're alone too much."

I smiled. My dad's ever-present concern was comforting.

"We'll probably be working here sometimes, so don't freak out if you see his truck in the driveway."

"His truck?" Dad smirked, spreading jelly on his toast. "You got paired with a boy?"

"Yeah?" I rolled my eyes. "We didn't get to pick our partners."

He chuckled to himself. He was probably imagining lovebirds flying overhead. I decided not to burst his bubble.

"I won't freak out over a truck in the drive." He polished off his toast and took his plate to the sink. "It's one of the perks of having a trustworthy daughter."

A few moments later, I was off to school and dad was settled in his easy chair with the newspaper. If nothing else in Sky Cove was okay, I at least had my dad.

***

I loved invisibility. I hadn't always felt that way, of course, but over time I'd learned that it was far better to be invisible than a target. So, I was thankful for each day that I could walk the halls of Sky Cove Senior High and not be noticed.

I'd mastered the art of being as nondescript as the used-to-be-white-but-now-they're-gray floors and long-ago-faded-paint-jobs on the classroom walls.

I almost made it the whole day with my invisibility in tact. Ironically enough, it was just outside the art room when I found myself in the spotlight.

Miller and a couple of his buddies huddled together in the hallway, most certainly solving the problems of the world.

The combination of football sweatshirts, testosterone, and self-righteousness was nauseating.

"You can't seriously want to stay in this class with crazies like her." This came from the meathead known as Shane London, a senior who used more gel on his black hair that most girls. He said the word *crazies* and gestured toward me without even attempting to hide the fact he was insulting me.

It took real talent to be both mean and stupid simultaneously.

"I talked to Mr. Brunswick. He said he could fit you in the weight-lifting class even though it's technically full." Meathead number two was Collin Wells, another senior who was nearly six and a half feet tall. I liked to think maybe that's why his elevator didn't go all the way to the top. "You know you want out of this place before any of the weird rubs off on you."

Collin seemed oblivious to the fact that he was insulting me and my fellow art geeks. I figured it didn't matter much. Thoughtless insults were just as hurtful as ones hurled on purpose.

Miller shrugged his shoulders and started to laugh. Then he saw me. For a brief moment our eyes made contact, and in his I saw something that might've almost been regret.

I wondered what he saw in mine.

It should've been no big surprise. So why did I feel sharp disappointment? Had I really thought he'd behave any differently?

Anger welled inside me. The sense of betrayal I felt made my face flame, my cheeks hot from the redness creeping across. I couldn't understand why. It had long since ceased to matter what other people said about me. It did no good to care about their opinions.

And besides, how had Miller betrayed me, when he'd done nothing but act exactly as he always did?

Shaking my head and ordering myself to get a grip, I walked into the room and took my seat. I didn't even blink when Miller sat next to me a minute later.

"Sorry about that."

I said nothing. Just reached in my pocket and pulled out the supply list and handed it to him.

"Hopefully each group has been able to talk about the project and make some plans," Miss Stockton said, beginning class with her usual breezy smile and sing-song voice.. Today she wore a frilly red skirt that hung to her ankles with a black cardigan sweater over a mustard yellow shirt. It didn't exactly clash, but it didn't exactly match either. As always, it worked on her. The ever-present red stone pendant dangled against the yellow of her shirt. "So that's what I want to hear about today. What are your plans?"

She went around the room and asked each pair of students what ideas they had. Several photography projects and one painting later she got to Todd and me.

"A high relief sculpture," I began. "Showing what the harbor used to look like years ago. Each piece will be separate, and we'll mount them all onto a large flat surface."

"Sounds lovely," she said, jotting things down in her notebook.

Standing this close, I had a good view of her necklace. I'd always been sort of fascinated by it, and looking at it now I could see the intricate carving on the silver metal that encased the stone. The swirly silver almost looked like long, delicate fingers wrapped around the red stone, as if guarding it.

Someday I'd ask her to let me take a closer look.

You choose to deny...

The words sang in my mind, uninvited. I hadn't thought them. I had no idea where they'd come from, but I knew the voice that spoke them. It was the same voice from my dream, lyrical and smooth, and yet filled with a pain so deep I felt it in my own heart, so intense I felt on the verge of crying.

Slamming my eyes shut, I rubbed my temples that now throbbed with insistent pain. I could not handle anything else crazy happening to me.

The bell rang, ending the school day, and snapping me out of my funk. I grabbed my backpack off the floor, wanting to get out of there quickly in case Miller's friends decided to make another appearance.

"I'll pick up the stuff on the list," Todd said, holding the paper I'd given him.

I nodded. "I'll reimburse you for half. You should be able to get it all at Pierce's. No need to go to the big store in Camden."

I started toward the door. He followed.

"Will you be on Facebook tonight?"

What the...?

"I don't know. I don't use it all that much."

"Well, I'll be on. Maybe we can talk."

I stopped and looked at him, and the incredulous look on my face must've been obvious, because he tacked on, "About the project."

I reminded myself that what I'd witnessed in the hallway before class was nothing new and in no way a surprise, so it was stupid to hold it against Todd. So he'd been dumped in art class because weight lifting was full? That kind of thing happened, and we did, after all, have to cooperate.

"If I have time," I answered.

I was halfway to my car when my phone buzzed, alerting a text message.

Miller.

My friends r dumb. I dropped weight lifting on purpose. Wanted 2 try something new.

Well.

Chapter 6

The thought of going home alone didn't sit well with me for some reason. Too many mixed up feelings I couldn't put names on. After leaving my dad a voicemail letting him know I wasn't going straight home, I headed toward the harbor, even though it wasn't ideal, with snow on the ground and the freezing temps.

At least the wind had given us a break today.

I came here from time to time when my mind was full and crowded. The serenity of the harbor, even in the winter calmed me.

The Sky Cove harbor was tiny compared to the one in Camden, but that's what I liked most about it... its quaintness.

Layering up with my heavy parka over my sweatshirt, I cinched the hood around my face and pulled on a pair of gloves, fingers of the right glove clipped off, of course. I sat in my favorite spot, a bench on a small hill overlooking the southern end of the harbor. Still not quite sure what had driven me here today, I pulled my ever-present sketchpad from my backpack.

Sketching wasn't my first choice, but it was a "do

anywhere" kind of thing, whereas carving required a little more prep. And sometimes, when I just needed to create, the sketchpad was a lifesaver.

Pencil in hand, I started to draw. As always, it began with just lines. Random shapes and shading. Whatever pleased me, even if it meant nothing, wound up on the paper. As my pencil moved, I let the weirdness of the past few days play through my mind. Miller's odd, but not necessarily bad, behavior. The crazy episodes I'd experienced after carving the small forest animals. The dream, which wasn't so much scary as it was confusing. The voice in my head during art class.

The water lapped gently in the distance, inspiring lots of curves and swirls, until the image on my paper began to look like the willowy fingers I'd seen on Miss Stockton's pendant.

Strange, but okay. Going with the flow I used cross-hatching to add texture and create shadows. The swirls in the center of the pendant turned into intricate patterns and knots.

Then my pencil took off, moving almost of its own volition. I loved it when creativity exploded like this. When the pencil seemed to be in control and I was just the vehicle for something greater.

And then she was there again. I wasn't surprised when the figure of my dream woman began to appear on the page. She was tall, willowy, her long hair cascading in beautiful waves over her shoulder, obscuring her face as it fell to her waist. The bell-shaped sleeves of her gown draped off her wrists in a most feminine way. A few swipes of my pencil and she stood alone in a forest, peaceful and whimsical.

I wondered who she was. What she was thinking. And from where did the inspiration for her come?

The sounds of passing cars drew me from the image, and I realized almost an hour had passed. The sunlight had started to fade into the hazy stuff that stretched between daylight and nightfall.

Add to that, my nose was an ice cube and my fingers

were numb.

I hated winter. I bemoaned the fact that sunlight was such a rare commodity as I closed up my sketchbook and packed up to leave. Not only was sunlight an artist's best friend, it also went a long way toward lifting the spirits.

Endless gray, colorless days didn't do much for my psyche. They just seemed so long, and the longer the day, the more I had to endure.

With one melancholy gaze at my mystery woman, I packed up my supplies and headed for my car.

There weren't a lot of people hanging out at the harbor today, for obvious reasons, so the man standing across the parking area was a surprise. He didn't even have a coat on. Just stood there looking across at me.

From this distance, I couldn't really see his face. The baseball cap pulled low hid him even further. I felt his gaze more than I saw it. Which was somehow even worse.

I didn't recognize him. And I didn't like his glare. Creeped out, I hurried to my car, threw my backpack into the passenger seat and took off.

Yes, I much preferred invisibility.

***

At home in my studio, I worked on the maquette for the harbor sculpture. Using random colors of cardstock for the individual shapes, the end product wound up looking like a huge package of Skittles had exploded.

I liked it.

I finished the rest of my homework with no real trouble, then re-packed my backpack and set it beside the door, ready to grab on my way out the next morning.

Dinner was a re-heat of spaghetti from last night, and I ate at the kitchen table alone, like I always did on school nights. I didn't mind it. Never had. I liked the solitude, the quiet.

I liked to think of myself as sensible and practical.

Settling on the brown plaid couch I surfed the satellite guide hoping for re-runs of *Criminal Minds*. I could use a dose of Dr. Spencer Reid. He was so my type. Most girls drooled over the over-muscled and over-confident Derek Morgan. But not me. Give me brains over brawn any day.

Sensible and practical.

Dr. Reid was nowhere to be found on my television, so I settled for *Teen Mom*, a guilty pleasure I'd never tell anyone about.

Will you be on Facebook tonight?

My eyes cut toward the studio where the light from my screensaver spilled through the open doorway. Why had Todd's words popped into my head all of a sudden?

And no, I was absolutely not going in there for my laptop.

I got up.

Grumbling the whole way.

I did not, however, bring the power cord. That would be my excuse to get off the computer, should I need one.

Oh I'm sorry Todd I've got to go. My battery's about to die?

Plopping back on the couch, I eyed the dove gray walls with suspicion, as if they might somehow tell my secret, and congratulated myself on my clever plan.

Logging in, I told myself he would not be there. Sure, he'd said he would, but guys like him said a lot of things. And anyway, it wasn't like he was going to be sitting home, waiting for me to log into Facebook.

I had an inbox message.

It was from Todd, letting me know he'd picked up the supplies.

There were a couple of wall posts as well, both from Tyler Thomas, who was also in the advanced art class. He and I were on the same level, both socially and artistically. However, he'd managed to get partnered with a sophomore girl who seemed oblivious to his uncoolness and was somewhat enamored with him.

He asked if I was doing okay. I was certain this was in

reference to being paired with Miller. I assured him via a response to his wall post that I was fine.

And I was. Really.

The chat box popped up.

Todd: *You gonna talk to me?*

Me: *About?*

Todd: *The project. Or whatever.*

The "or whatever" worried me.

Me: *I did a maquette of it this afternoon.*

Todd: *A what?*

Me: *Like a model of it. Out of paper. So we can see sort of what it'll look like when it's finished.*

Todd: *Oh. Cool.*

Me: *I guess you're going to have to come over here to work on it though. All my tools are here.*

Todd: *OK. I picked up the supplies on the list. I could bring them by tomorrow after school.*

Me: *I figured you'd have basketball practice.*

Todd: *Not playing basketball this year.*

Curious. For the past three years he'd been the star of the football team and a big name on the basketball team, too. I supposed that was part of his allure. A two-sport athlete meant people fell all over themselves to accommodate you.

Me: *How come?*

Todd: *Don't like it. Never did. My dad wanted me to play. That's part of why he's pissed at me, because I didn't play this year.*

Interesting.

Me: *You like football right?*

Todd: *Yeah. It comes natural.*

My dad had never wanted me to be anything other than who I was. So, I didn't have crap to deal with at home on top of what went on at school. I wondered how much of Todd was a product of his dad's insistence.

Also curious was Miller's forthcomingness online. How odd that he could seem so normal and down-to-earth on Facebook, and yet so full of himself in person.

Something rumbled outside, like a truck approaching. My

dad wouldn't be home for a while, and traffic on Cliffhaven Lane this time of night was unusual. There were only two houses beyond ours, both of them retired married couples.

Setting the laptop on the floor, I walked to the front window. Through the sheer curtain I saw lights of some kind, and the outline of a vehicle sitting still on the road in front of our house. I pulled the curtain back.

The darkness wouldn't allow me to see inside the cab of huge flatbed truck. I couldn't tell if the driver was male or female, old or young. But somehow I knew that whoever was in that truck was looking right at me.

The truck didn't move. It was like some sort of staring contest. I didn't care in the least if I won.

I dropped the curtain back in place and stepped away from the window. I could still see lights, but nothing else.

The truck's engine revved. Once. Twice. Three times, as if trying to get my attention or send a message. Then the lights moved and the truck sped down the street.

I was not paranoid, but that was just unnerving. Looking at the clock, I realized it would be an hour before my dad got home from work, and after that, I wasn't crazy about the idea of going to sleep without him here.

Suddenly, I wasn't in a big hurry to log off Facebook.

Me: *Your parents care how late you stay on here?*

Todd: *Nah. Dad's not even home.*

Me: *Cool. Let's talk then.*

CHAPTER 7

The next morning on the way to school, I debated the wisdom of the lengthy conversation Miller and I had online. We chatted for over an hour, until I heard my dad pull in the driveway, and it felt completely surreal the whole time.

In my head I knew I was talking to Miller, the shallow, superficial jock. But it hadn't seemed that way while we talked. He'd seemed almost normal.

He didn't talk a lot about himself, other than to say that he and his dad stayed at odds with each other most of the time. When he mentioned his mom a couple of times, a touch of affection came through, even though it was only words in the chat box.

And apparently he really had dropped weightlifting on purpose. Since he wasn't playing basketball he'd wanted a break from the guys he lifted with. He said they were constantly on his nerves these days.

I had to give him a point or two for that.

But I could not afford to soften up toward him. He was still Miller, if a little less of an idiot. It was only a matter of time before he returned to his regular self.

But, I decided that for the time being, it was okay to

enjoy the fact that he didn't totally repulse me.

Pulling into my parking spot, I grabbed my backpack and trudged through the parking lot while snow flurried, whipping around in the nasty wind that blustered about. Halfway there, I ran into Layla Bradford, the girl who'd moved in last semester and was now dating Lucas Ellis. It was really quite the scandal, the new girl with no social connections landing the most sought-after boy in the school. But Layla was really nice, and so was Lucas, and they were really happy together.

For once, the good girl finished first, and the normal hierarchy of popularity did not.

"Hi Phoebe," she said, pulling up next to me as if I were just another regular girl at Sky Cove Senior High.

I liked the feeling, even though I told myself it wasn't important.

"Hey Layla," I answered. "Liking the winter here?"

She'd moved from Tennessee. If I hated the winters here, it was probably pretty brutal for her.

"It's something else." She laughed. "I've never seen so much snow. I guess I'm just too happy to be bothered too much by the freezing cold."

Yeah, she was happy. It showed, and I was glad for her. She was kind to me when very few others were.

When we got to the door, it opened for us. Miller was on the other side.

"Thanks Todd." Layla gave him a smile he probably didn't deserve if the rumor about the first day of school was true, and I figured it probably was. I'd heard that Miller made fun of her name in a rather sexual manner in front of a crowd of people. Good thing for him Layla seemed the forgiving type.

"No problem." He nodded toward Layla. "Hey Phoebe."

Layla and I turned toward the hallway, heading toward our lockers. Lucas appeared and fell into step next to Layla at the same time Todd walked up beside me.

I could feel the stares from everywhere. Uncomfortable

didn't begin to describe it. Todd walking beside me was completely screwing with my invisibility.

Layla and Lucas stopped at her locker, whispering in that goofy way couples had. My first thought was *yuck,* but then I decided it was probably nice to have someone you trusted that much. Someone who looked at you that way.

Not that I'd know. Or even needed to know.

"So," Todd began as I worked the combination on my locker. "After school, right?"

A small crowd gathered near the water fountain across the hall. The hush-toned snickering commenced. I could hear the OMGs and WTFs. Great. Just great. First thing in the morning and I was the object of everyone's attention.

I nodded, hoping he'd just go away. I knew he didn't have a class in this hallway, so surely he needed to get to first period.

"I guess since our last class is together I can just follow you," he went on. "That okay?"

"It's fine," I snapped. He looked at me with narrowed eyes, and I sort of felt bad for my tone. But could he not tell what was happening? Surely he didn't want to be seen talking to me.

"Hey Miller, you slumming it?"

I didn't even turn around to see who said it.

"Shut the hell up Lance."

Ah, Lance something-or-other. The short kid with jet-black hair who always made wisecracks to make up for his lack of height.

Figured.

***

I tried to muster up an appropriate level of nonchalance the entire drive home.

After the incident with Lance, my day had been thankfully uneventful, and yet the exchange still ran through my mind.

Hey Miller, you slumming it?
Shut the hell up, Lance.

It confounded me that Todd hadn't just agreed with Lance and laughed it off.

After all, he could legitimately claim he was being forced to work with me. It would certainly be better for his reputation.

And why was I concerned with his reputation?

Geez, could I over-analyze the situation any more?

Todd's words to Lance were probably just his way of intimidating the little jerk into not messing with him anymore, and had nothing to do with him being upset that I'd been insulted.

Part of me hated that I expected so little of Miller, but he did have a habit of living down to everyone's expectations. Although, I had to admit, there were moments over the past couple of days when I'd begun to hope for a little more.

Perhaps my cynicism was decreasing.

I watched in the rearview mirror as his truck turned on to Cliffhaven Lane. It was all business from here on out. Unloading supplies, planning our work sessions, and setting a deadline for finishing. No more thinking about Todd Miller and his motivations.

***

"So we're working tomorrow after school?" I asked, stacking the last of the wood against the far wall of my studio.

We'd taken the maquette of the project and matched each piece with the wood that would be used to carve it and created a schedule for the next couple of weeks. However, before he left, I felt compelled to remind him of our next appointment.

His phone rang before he could answer me, some heavy rap song sounding from his jeans pocket. He looked at the screen and stepped out into the living room, his whole demeanor screaming tension.

"Mom?" I didn't want to eavesdrop, since he'd obviously stepped out of the room for some privacy, but he wasn't exactly lowering his voice to keep me from hearing. "What did you find out?"

Results? Obviously something was wrong.

"Okay," he said, his voice flat, and his shoulders tense as if a weight had settled on them.

"I'll see you when I get home." The affection in his voice was obvious as he walked back in the studio, although worry stewed in his eyes.

When I saw the phone go back in his pocket, I asked about tomorrow again.

When he didn't respond, I turned around.

He stood at my desk, staring at the fox and lynx carvings next to my computer.

He hadn't heard me.

"Todd," I said, walking toward him. "Tomorrow, right?"

He raised his head and blinked several times.

"Sorry. Yeah, tomorrow." He looked back at the animals. "Did you make these?"

"Yes," I said. "For an art scholarship I'm applying for."

"When?"

"The scholarship?"

"No. When did you make these?"

I didn't answer immediately. Why did he care when I'd carved the fox and the lynx?

"I'm just curious," he said, clearly noticing my perplexed look. "They look like they'd take a long time to get them that life-like."

I shrugged. "Not really. But then, carving comes easy to me. I did the fox last week, and the lynx a couple of nights ago."

I swore I saw panic flash through his eyes, but the next instant it was gone, replaced by a blank gaze.

"I've got to go." He grabbed his jacket from the back of the chair and was out the door before I could even say

39

goodbye.

So much for manners!

And what was with that look of panic when talking about the fox and the lynx? How could two small carvings possibly cause such panic?

Then I remembered what I'd experienced when carving those animals, and the blood drained from my face. Suddenly cold, I recalled the out-of-body-visions-of-the-forest stuff. I shook my head. No way. It was impossible. I'd chalked those hallucinations up to over-active imagination anyway.

He couldn't be connected to it.

But the look on Todd's face...

No, no, no. The thought was just too preposterous. No freaking way was it possible.

There was one way to know for certain.

Closing my eyes and taking a shaky breath, I took a piece of scrap maple and my V-tool, and sat down at my desk to work.

I took my time carving the small black bear. I wanted to pay close attention to each thought, each feeling as the young animal began to come to life in my hands. My lack of haste also had to do with the fact that if what I suspected was true, Miller needed to be home and out from behind the wheel of his truck before I finished.

For a moment I worried about his parents, and what would happen if *something* happened in front of them, but if he was involved in this insanity, it seemed as though he'd had enough warning each time to get outside before... whatever.

Finally giving attention the bear's face, I felt the edges of my vision begin to shift. My gaze met the tiny eyes emerging from the wood in my hands. My senses sharpened as I made the conscious effort to connect with... whatever it was.

Footsteps. A door opening, then closing. Familiar sounds. A sense of urgency and uncertainty. I felt it all as my sight narrowed, focusing into a tiny dot until I no longer saw what was in front of me.

Instead of my studio, I now saw gray haze, misty like fog. Then finally a clearing. The scene somewhat familiar. The edge of a wooded area, same as before.

Frantic. That was the only word to describe the emotion running through us. As frightening as these episodes had been for me, I couldn't begin to imagine what it must be like on his end.

Could he hear me? Feel me?

Did he get this crazy connection? Did he know he wasn't alone?

Todd, can you hear me?

Kind of a stupid question, since I didn't say the words out loud. It was more like I just aimed the thought at him.

I felt the eyes dart from side to side, as if looking for the source of the voice... or the thought or whatever it was.

I know this is insane. But I'm here too.

The frenzied feelings began to calm, just a bit, and we settled behind the same tree where we'd taken refuge the last time. Even as we sat quietly, I could feel the questions running through him.

How? Why? Can we stop it?

He wasn't used to feeling helpless, and I could feel his frustration.

I searched my mind, even as I stared out at the floor of the forest with its patches of snow and fallen limbs. I could still picture myself as I actually was, sitting in my studio. What had pulled me out of the visions before? Perhaps if our connection could be broken, the craziness would stop for him too.

I recalled the sound of my dad coming in the front door, and the sound of the lynx falling from my hand and hitting the floor. Sound! Both times it had been external sound that halted the hallucination or vision or fugue... or whatever this was.

Hang on. I think I can make it stop.

I relaxed my hands, which proved much more difficult

than I thought, given that I was currently not *in* the room, but rather in some screwed up alternate dimension. As I forced the muscles to go lax, I felt the animal and the carving knife slip.

The split second it took for the objects to hit the floor seemed like a year. When they finally clanked against the floor, the fog began to lift, and the scene in front of my eyes began to return to normal.

Before it faded completely, I sent him one last thought.

Tomorrow.

CHAPTER 8

I worried about last period all day. How, exactly, did one go about interacting normally with someone they'd communicated with via some crazy-psychic-connection-thingy?

Somehow, I figured "So Todd, what was it like being a bear?" was not the right approach.

Normal. I had to act normal. Who knew if Miller would even acknowledge what had happened. I mean, it's not like it was every day your realities shifted so completely. I was having enough trouble grasping it myself. It might take him some time to wrap his brain around everything.

He walked into the art room just as I sat down. It was the first time I'd seen him all day. I wasn't surprised that he hadn't met me at the door first thing this morning. Actually, I was relieved he hadn't.

I guess we both needed some distance.

"Hey." He sounded tired.

"Hi."

"So, we still on for this afternoon?"

I nodded.

So did he.

Sparkling conversation, for sure.

Miss Stockton started class, effectively ending the painful exchange, and I was glad. But just because the conversation between us stopped did not mean the awkwardness did. Based on Todd's fidgeting and the constant tapping of his foot, his discomfort at being in the seat next to me was obvious. I had little doubt he'd experienced what I had the night before.

Which meant my suspicions were accurate. Todd had turned into a bear – and a fox and a lynx – after I'd carved them. So what did that make him? Some kind of shape shifter or were-creature?

And what did the fact that somehow I saw what he saw during these crazy episodes make me?

And how in the world was any of this even remotely possible?

My life had become a SyFy movie.

***

"Want something to drink?" I asked, unlocking the front door. Todd had followed me home, just as we'd planned, and I hoped to ease the tension between us. "Soft drinks are in the fridge."

"Thanks," he muttered, and walked over to the refrigerator.

I dropped my coat and backpack on the floor, made my way to the studio, and began pulling out the supplies I'd need for today's session.

According to the schedule we'd made yesterday, we were supposed to be cutting the large pieces that would become the water and the hillside, as they were the foundation upon which the smaller carvings would be mounted, but at the last minute I decided to switch it up.

Sitting down at my work table, I pulled out my carving tools and a smaller block of wood, thinking it might be better to do a carving of one of the small houses, and just let

Todd watch. He didn't seem in the mood to be actively involved. Maybe he'd rather just watch me carve instead.

I unzipped my hoodie and hung it on the back of my chair, revealing my yellow tee shirt and jeans. Much more exposed than I wanted to be in front of him, but I couldn't carve with the oversized hoodie sleeves in my way.

A second later he stepped into the room with two cans of Lemon lime soda.

"Thought you might like one, too," he said, and a somewhat pleasant expression crossed his face.

"Thank you." I smiled at him, thankful that the anxiety between us seemed a little less.

I took the ponytail holder out of my hair and grabbed the clip I always kept handy in my studio. It took me all of three seconds to wad my hair on the top of my head and clip it into place. I couldn't do detailed work with my ponytail falling over my shoulder.

Looking back at Todd, I found him staring. "I never realized how long you hair is."

I felt the heat creep into my cheeks, but it wasn't from embarrassment. I think in his own way, he'd just complimented me. I had no idea how to handle compliments. Especially from a guy.

I wanted to tell him that I kept it in a ponytail all the time because my hair didn't matter and no one cared what I looked like anyway, but that would've revealed way too much.

All that came out was a squeaky, "It gets in my way."

Thankfully, he let the subject drop.

"So what's first today?" he asked, pulling a chair next to mine.

I turned to look at him and saw him cut his eyes toward my computer. I figured he'd look for the small animals, so I'd purposely put them out of sight. If the right moment presented itself, I'd show them to him later.

"I'm thinking we should jump ahead," I began. "We can do the big cutting another day. Why don't I carve something small and show you how it works?"

One corner of his mouth lifted. My heart did a crazy little flip. He was pleased that I was going to let him watch me carve. And I was pleased that he wanted to watch.

That it made me happy almost pissed me off. Almost.

"Sounds good." He took a swig of his drink, smiled again. "I'd like that."

I smiled back, even though I didn't want to, and felt the shell I'd spent years building around myself soften just the slightest bit.

Afraid to say anything for fear something sweet and mushy might come flying out, I picked up the piece of wood and a carving knife and went to work.

Silent, Todd just watched. I felt his presence beside me like a warm fire, pleasant and comforting. I switched from the carving knife to the gouge then to the v-tool, each time explaining the different purposes of each tool.

"It's called subtractive sculpture because we're taking material away in order to make the figure," I said as I used the chisel to begin adding details to the roof of the little house.

As the recognizable features began to take shape, Todd leaned closer, propping his elbows on the top of the metal table I used when working. He seemed both fascinated and apprehensive. I barely kept myself from chuckling when I realized he was probably wondering if he was going to turn into a house.

It took about an hour to get to a stopping point. I could do the finishing touches later. I set the little house on the table and stretched my arms.

"Hard work, huh?" he asked.

"Not so much. I mean, sure it takes time and effort, but it doesn't seem like hard work when I enjoy it."

"I wouldn't have the first idea how to begin to do something like that."

He was impressed. And I was flattered.

Good Lord, what was wrong with me that his opinion

now meant something?

"I wouldn't have the first idea how to run a football play either."

He smiled. "I'll teach you about football if you want."

"Cool," I said, gathering my tools to put them back into the box. "Maybe I'll actually watch the Superbowl next month."

I had never said anything so goofy in my life. Me, watch the Superbowl? What did I care about big dumb oafs running into each other and piling into huge heaps of bodies as they chased a stupid ball? Like I'd ever be interested in...

Without warning, he touched my hand. I felt his skin against mine, soft and light, as I closed my carving tools up. The jolt of electricity that went through me at the contact was foreign and strange and wonderful all at once.

I didn't know what to do. Was I supposed to say something? Look at him? I had absolutely no clue what the proper reaction was.

"Phoebe", he said, his voice whispery and nice.

I looked at him then, totally unprepared for the expression I saw on his face.

He leaned toward me.

Emotions I couldn't identify barreled through me, welling in the pit of my stomach and radiating outward until my whole body felt alive.

Then his lips touched mine.

The shock paralyzed me. I should stop him, push him away, and slap him across the face for kissing me, but I did none of those things.

I just sat there, like a star-struck idiot, kissing him back.

My very first kiss. And it was with Todd Miller.

I wanted to be upset about it.

I wasn't.

I hated myself in that moment.

When he pulled back to look at me, I braced for some sort of remark that would trivialize what he'd just done. I mean, if his previous bragging could be believed, he'd done his fair share of kissing and lots more, and surely I was just another name on the list now.

But he surprised me. Again.

"This is the real you," he whispered, his big hands framing my face. "The girl that comes alive in this studio. The girl whose face lights up when she's creating. That's the real you."

I would not nod my head. I would not nod my head. I would not nod my head.

I nodded.

"Why do you hide yourself from everyone at school?"

"No one cares who I am." The honesty left my mouth without my consent, and I wanted desperately to pull the words back inside.

"They might," he said, thumbs moving in circles on my cheeks. "If you let them see you."

I scooted back from him, with effort. I didn't want the warm feelings that he created in me. I didn't want the sense of closeness that swirled around us.

I refused them.

"Why should I?" I turned my back to him and grabbed my hoodie, quickly zipping it up. "Why should I go to any effort for the idiots at school? All they've ever done is judge me, pigeon-hole me as the skanky girl, the grungy freak. They made me this way, so why should I try to be any different? They'd just find another reason to dislike me."

"You're right." His agreement shocked me, almost as much as the kiss. "I just wish people could see the real you. I wish I had."

Whatever. I could not afford to entertain the notion that Todd Miller somehow liked me. The consequences of such idiocy could be disastrous.

I walked over to my desk, thinking I'd just get the small animals out of the drawer and show him what I'd carved last night. Yeah, that should throw ice cubes on whatever he thought he was going to accomplish by cozying up to me.

Except, when I glanced over at him, he looked so

peaceful. And darn it all, he was still smiling at me.

Though a part of me wanted to shock him into stupid silence with what I'd discovered, a bigger part of me didn't have the heart to do it. At least not yet.

CHAPTER 9

"Art project going okay?" my dad asked, the next morning over breakfast. I smiled. He always remembered what I had going on.

I nodded, hoping that would be the end of it. I didn't want to talk about Miller. I didn't want to think about Miller. I didn't want to think about the fact that underneath my hoodie was a girly-pink shirt, or the fact that my hair was not in a ponytail... yet. The hair band was around my wrist, just in case I changed my mind.

No such luck. Dad plowed on with the conversation while he stirred sugar into his coffee.

"Who's the partner you're working with?"

I sighed. No getting around it.

"Todd Miller." I didn't look up from my cereal.

"Miller? His dad the one who owns the construction business?"

I shrugged. I really had no idea.

"The kid's a football player, right?"

"Yeah."

"That's the one, then."

I'd replayed the events of yesterday afternoon over and

over again in my mind, much to my own dismay. I didn't want to spend energy thinking about kissing Miller, but apparently I had no control over my thoughts.

Whatever it had seemed like yesterday, I knew it meant nothing. At least to him. And I could make it mean nothing to me, too. Just because it was my first kiss didn't mean it had to be significant or important.

So why had I gone to the trouble of finding something feminine to put on? And why had I taken the time to make sure my hair looked decent out of a ponytail.

Because I was freaking stupid, that's why.

"He being helpful?" dad asked. "Talk around town is he doesn't work too hard at anything besides sports."

Overcome with the urge to defend him, my eyes shot to my dad's. I caught myself just before I opened my mouth. What was with the jump-up-and-be-Miller's-champion compulsion?

Still, I couldn't let my dad think Miller was slacking. Because really, he wasn't.

"He's fine," I answered. "He's being helpful."

I left out that part of his helpfulness involved sucking face. I figured Dad wouldn't appreciate that.

I wasn't sure I appreciated it.

But I couldn't deny I didn't hate it.

Sheesh, what a mess. As if these crazy visions of mine, and Todd morphing into wild animals weren't enough, I had to be all conflicted about my feelings for him.

It was so much easier when he was a big dumb jerk. If I could just go back to disliking him on principle...

Then I remembered what he'd looked like after the kiss, all sweet and smiling, and somehow I knew that was a moment I couldn't give up.

My spoon clanked against the bottom of the bowl as I finished my cereal, lost in thought. I ordered myself to stop obsessing about Miller. I put my dishes in the dishwasher, kissed my dad goodbye, and headed out the door. With any luck, I wouldn't see Miller until last period.

***

No one even blinked at the six new inches of snow that fell overnight. Such was winter in Maine. Once the snow started, we didn't see a snow-free ground again until March, if then. The snowplows were forever in use, so it was no surprise that the school parking lot was cleared.

Miller's truck was in its usual spot, but he was nowhere to be seen. Not that I was looking for him.

Entering the building, I navigated my way through the crowd of kids in the lobby, finally emerging in the hallway. The bright red lockers were a strange contrast to the dull gray floors and walls, which I thought made a nice metaphor for this place. A few bright spots in a vast sea of ordinary. A couple of students stood around the water fountain area, but for the most part, the hall was empty.

At my locker, I unloaded my heavy coat, but kept the hoodie on. I was still undecided about removing it. My hair, void of the usual ponytail, stayed tucked inside my sweatshirt. Still unsure about that too.

"No ponytail today?" The question came from Layla.

I showed her the band on my wrist. "Not yet, anyway."

"You look different," she said. "And it's not just the hair."

I shrugged. Truth was, I felt sort of different, and I didn't really know if I liked it or not.

Rummaging through my backpack for the essentials I needed for my next class, my sketchbook fell open to the picture I'd sketched at the harbor the other day. For a moment I left the present and stood in the forest with the woman from my sketch. I felt the happiness that swirled inside her, coupled with an uncertainty that hovered over her joy.

Her feelings closely mirrored my own.

And how in the heck did I know what the woman felt? She wasn't even real. She was a figment of my imagination...

or of my sketch pencil.

"Phoebe?" Layla's hand lightly touched my shoulder. "You okay?"

How long had I been lost in the forest? Cutting my eyes left and right, I noted that most kids still lingered in the hallway, exactly as they had been before the sketch pulled me in. Hopefully I'd not zoned out for more than a couple of seconds.

"Sorry," I said, blinking to bring the real world back into focus. "Just distracted, I guess."

Layla just looked at me, a speculative expression on her face. No doubt she'd heard about the uneasy partnership between Miller and me. She probably wondered if my funk had anything to do with him.

"You ever have déjà vu?" I asked, hoping that would keep the conversation from steering toward Miller.

Layla's eyes widened and she dropped her gaze to my open sketchbook, as if she somehow knew exactly what I meant.

"Yeah," she said. "I have."

The warning bell rang and saved me from having to explain my comment about déjà vu. I closed my locker with a satisfying slam, said a quick goodbye Layla, and headed off to start my day.

And in the back of my mind I wondered if I was losing my mind.

***

I stopped at my locker just before last period. I couldn't decide if I was glad the day hadn't drug on and on or sorry that it had gone by so quickly. My hair was still ponytail-less, failing to my shoulder blades. Before I could think about all the reasons why I shouldn't, I took off my hoodie and draped it over my arm, leaving me in baggy jeans a pink long-sleeve tee. Pulling my backpack from the locker, I turned and headed for the art room.

Rounding the corner into the lobby and preparing to take another right turn into the next hallway, I caught sight of Todd.

And stopped cold.

He hadn't seen me yet, and no wonder. He was all wrapped up in Tina Parker, one of the cheerleading bobbleheads who walked around school like they were God's gift to spandex.

I should go... just turn and go to class and chalk this up to a lesson well learned. But instead, I just stood there, watching as Tina played with the collar of Miller's shirt and his arm snaked around her back pulling her closer to him. Beside him, Shane and Collin carried on what was surely a deep and intelligent conversation with Erica Moore, another of the bobbleheads.

Wasn't this just perfect? The football jocks and the cheerleaders, all cozied up in the hallway. Could there be a bigger stereotype anywhere in this school? And here I stood, no hoodie and hair down, feeling like a fool a hundred times over.

I took a step toward the next hallway, and that was when he saw me. The color drained from his face and all kinds of regret and apology crossed his expression. My cheeks burned, and so did my eyes, but I would not give in to any sort of weakness. However lousy I felt inside, no way was Todd Miller going to see it.

Instead, I just shook my head, in an I-should've-known sort of gesture, and turned away.

I didn't run down the hall. I didn't even walk fast. That would've given too much away. I just made my way to the art room, took out my hair band and put my hair up, slipped on my hoodie, and zipped it all the way up. By the time Miller got to the room and took his seat, I looked exactly like I usually did.

And things between us had returned to the status quo. Something inside me ached at the knowledge. Again, I reminded myself that such behavior was simply par for the course for Miller. He couldn't be counted on for consistency or consideration. I should not have expected more.

But somehow, over the past several days, I'd done exactly that. I'd begun to expect more than he was capable of.

That was my mistake. One I wouldn't make again.

CHAPTER 10

I didn't wait for Miller after school. He knew the way to my house now, so he didn't need to follow me. Part of me hoped he'd just bail on the project today. It would save me from the awkwardness that was sure to happen if we were alone in the same room.

But no such luck. His truck pulled into my driveway just as I dropped my backpack. Quickly, I shot my dad a text and decided to just pretend nothing happened. I would go on about business as if he'd never kissed me. As if I'd never seen him flirting with Tina. As if we weren't experiencing insane, interconnected paranormal episodes.

He knocked, the rapping sound causing me to jump. Thankfully, I'd left the back door open so I could avoid having to open the door for him.

"It's open," I called from the studio.

The sound of his footsteps in the house sent waves of anxiety coursing through me, but I ignored them. I pulled out the large pieces of wood that would be cut today, and would eventually become the hillside and the water. If nothing else was going right in this stupid situation, I could at least make sure that the sculpture turned out perfect.

Though my back was to the door, I could tell when he stepped into the room. The air changed, became charged with his presence. The woodsy scent of his cologne reached me, nearly frying my resolve. I heard him remove his coat and walk toward me. With each step I imagined the excuses he was sure to make.

"Phoebe," he said.

"I figured we'd go ahead with the large piece today," I responded, not giving him a chance to finish whatever he was about to say. I scooted my worktable closer to my computer desk and placed an edge of the plywood on each, leaving the space beneath the middle empty. "It shouldn't take long, so we can get ourselves back on schedule."

"Phoebe, can we - "

I cut him off. "I've already freehanded the outline of the piece, so if you'll just hold the plywood still, I'll do the cutting with the handheld saw."

Removing the saw from the battery charger, I looked at him for the first time. *I'm sorry* was written all over his face. I could tell he wanted to explain, but I wasn't in the mood to hear it. The power tool in my hands deterred him from continuing.

Instead, I nodded toward the plywood. With a resigned sigh, he complied and held the piece of wood still while I cut.

It took a few minutes to complete. Precision was rarely quick. Afterward, I handed him a square of sandpaper to smooth out the edges, while I went to work carving a part of the rocky shoreline. We worked in silence, except for the scraping sound of the sandpaper, for which I was thankful. The tension still hung in the room like a thick fog.

After what seemed like forever, Todd laid the wood on the table and pulled his chair closer to me.

"Phoebe, I'm really sorry." His voice was soft and low, and so inviting I almost looked at him.

"For what?" I stopped myself from looking, trading the completed piece of shoreline for a small sailboat that needed a bit more detail. I refused to let him draw me into this exchange.

"For that shit with Tina."

I just shrugged my shoulders and kept working. I wondered if that's how he'd describe what happened with me yesterday. *That shit with Phoebe.*

"I don't blame you for not making this easy on me," he said. "But I really am sorry. I didn't mean for all that to happen."

I would not respond. I would not let him see me bothered by this. I would not stoop to pointing fingers.

"You didn't mean to put your arm around her and press her all up against you like velcro?"

Damn, I did stoop. Though I was furious with myself, I figured I'd already started, so why stop now. So I plowed right on.

"Or you didn't mean for me to see you?"

"It's not like that," he said. "I wasn't trying to sneak around, I just - "

"So you meant for me to see you? That makes it so much better."

"No, I didn't want any of that."

"Whatever. It's not like I care what you do or who you do it with."

"What do you mean you don't care?" He sounded on the edge of anger. "If you don't care then why are you mad?"

"Oh, so you want me to be mad?" I tossed the sailboat and the gouge onto the table and looked up at him, my eyes boring into his. "You wanted me to see you practically sharing a skin with Tina so I'd be mad? How sweet of you!"

"I didn't want you to see me with Tina!" he shouted. "I didn't want to be with Tina!"

"You could've fooled me."

"Damn it Phoebe, I'm trying to explain!"

"And doing a fine job of it."

"Just listen to me for a second." He stood up from the chair and shoved his hands through his hair, clearly frustrated. "Just shut up and listen to me."

I crossed my arms and just sat, pretending to be completely uninterested in what he had to say.

"I know you're pissed, and I don't blame you. And I know it matters even though you say it doesn't. You saw me in the hall with Tina and you wondered what the hell I was doing flirting with another girl after I kissed you yesterday. I'm well aware it made me look like a total ass."

In response, I raised my eyebrows.

"Tina and Erica came up and starting talking to Shane and Collin and me. At first it was just normal stuff, but then Tina got all flirty. I didn't want to respond to her, I swear. But Shane and Collin were there, and I knew they expected me to flirt back. The old me would've jumped right into it without a hesitation."

"The old you?"

"Yeah, the one who signed up for weightlifting," he said. "Not the one who dropped weightlifting to take art. They don't really understand why I've changed, and I don't know how to explain it to them. There are all these expectations on me, about how I should act and who I should like because of who I am."

"Oh, don't expect me to feel sorry for you because you're popular," I scoffed. "Poor little Todd Miller, he's so put-upon because he's popular. Boo freaking hoo."

"Just because I'm popular doesn't mean I have it easy."

"Looks easy from where I've been walking the past few years."

He stopped his pacing and looked at me. "I know it does. And I'm not saying you've had an easy go of it. I know you haven't. People, including me, have treated you like shit for no reason. And that sucks. It's not fair. I'm just saying that being popular isn't all that easy either. It comes with a set of rules that you have to keep."

"So today, with Tina, you were just 'keeping the rules', is that it?" I knew I sounded sarcastic. "I mean, it's not like you could tell her that you were interested in someone else, because for one thing you're not interested in me, and for another that would be against the rules."

"You've got your own set of rules," he said. "You hide under baggy clothes and walk around school looking at everybody and thinking how much better you are than the rest of us because you don't subscribe to the same set of rules. You may not be popular, but you're just as much of a snob."

My face burned and I opened my mouth to argue but realized I had no response. Good lord, could he be right?

"Reverse snobbery is still snobbery," he said.

I said nothing.

"I really am sorry." He sat down next to me again. "I'm trying to be different, for a lot of reasons, and I know I'm not going to get it right every time."

Okay, as far as honesty went his explanation was not bad, but I was just not prepared to go back to the way things had been.

"Okay," I said, rolling my chair back, putting a few more inches between us. I knew he was waiting for some sort of response from me, but that was the best I could do at the moment.

Besides, we had other things to deal with.

I walked over to my computer desk and opened the top drawer. I pulled out the three small animals, keeping them hidden in my hands.

Returning to the worktable, I sank back into my seat. "The other day you asked me about the little animals I'd carved."

I saw alarm move across his expression, but he masked it quickly. "Yeah."

"I carved another one," I said. "I thought you might want to see."

I laid the three figures carefully on the table in front of him. First the fox, then the lynx, and finally the bear.

CHAPTER 11

The silence settled in, like a dense, heavy fog. The walls of my studio seemed to close in, and oxygen was in short supply. Todd said nothing. He just stared at the animals on the table.

I found myself at a loss for words, too. Like maybe if we didn't say anything, if we refused to acknowledge it, it would all go away.

Then he looked at me, and the shock in his expression turned to confusion, then finally resignation.

"This is crazy," he whispered.

I nodded. My sentiments exactly.

"How?"

"I don't know." I shrugged my shoulders.

"What do you mean you don't know?" Surprise laced his voice. "You're the one doing this."

He couldn't actually think I was doing this on purpose. Could he?

"When I carved the fox, I thought I had some kind of hallucination or daydream or something. I was just as shocked as you."

He cut his eyes toward me. "I really doubt that. I turned

into a freaking animal. I thought I was dying. It felt like my insides were being crushed. You sit in here and carve."

I swallowed hard. His words sliced me up inside. I knew it had terrified him. I'd felt it.

"You're right," I said. "It's not as bad on my end. But it's not as easy as sitting in my studio carving. I think I see what you see. In fact, I can't see anything else. It's like the whole rest of the world drops away and I can only see what you see while you're - "

"Shape-shifting," Todd said, eliminating my phrasing problem.

"Thats sounds so bad," I whispered. "Can we call it something else?"

"Probably doesn't matter what we call it. It's still happening."

For lack of something to do, I shoved the animals back in the drawer, wishing that as I slammed it closed I could somehow put a stop to this.

"I won't carve any more." I could tell he was struggling, torn between being angry or confused. I figured it was best to just drop it for now, let it all settle in. If that was even possible. "We can just forget about all this."

Todd shook his head. "I don't think I'll be forgetting anytime soon. And I'm not going to stop wanting to know what the hell is going on."

I stood with my back to him for a moment, staring out the window on the back wall. The gray skies mirrored the anguish I felt in my heart. I'd begun the day anxious to see him, wondering what would happen after yesterday's kiss. After the incident in the hall, I'd been pissed off and hurt. Now I was just plain tired. And despite the fact that I was in this just as much as Todd, I felt sorry for him.

"I don't even know how to begin trying to figure out what's happening," I whispered, still not turning to look at him.

"Me either." His voice came from directly behind me. Somehow he'd moved close with out me realizing it. "But

I'm damn well going to try."

And then he left.

CHAPTER 12

Todd's abrupt departure weighed on me all night and into the next morning. There'd been no contact via Facebook that night. If Todd was online, he'd hidden himself so that no one else saw it. I texted him once and asked if he was okay. When he didn't respond, I promised myself I would not text again.

He was confused, scared, and pissed, and I understood all of that. And I knew he probably still thought that in some small way I'd intentionally done this to him.

I felt both dread and curiosity on my way to school. I had no idea how he'd act toward me, and I couldn't decide what would be worse - if he acted like I was garbage, which wouldn't actually be much different than he'd treated me before all this started, or if he acted like nothing at all had happened.

I went about my business, just like usual, but on my way to lunch, I encountered the meatheads and the bobbleheads.

"Maybe she thinks he's going to take her to prom," Tina said, earning a hearty laugh from Shane and Collin.

"Like that would ever happen," Erica added.

Since they were having their conversation right beside the

cafeteria doors, it was more than a little obvious they meant for me to hear them.

And... oh joy... Lance joined them.

"Stranger things have happened, my man," Lance said, slapping Shane on the back and sending a wink toward Erica. His brown eyes practically twinkling with joy as he continued to insult Todd. "Miller's been acting all strange lately, so who knows? Maybe he's decided to defect to the other side of the tracks."

God, he was such a jerk!

Suddenly, the bland aroma of steamed broccoli seemed welcoming. The double doors leading to the cafeteria beckoned like a long lost friend.

Refusing to be drawn into their stupid game, I tucked my chin to my chest and plowed right into the lunchroom. Layla walked in right behind me and said, "People in this school suck."

I chuckled, remembering when I'd said the same thing to her right after she'd moved here.

"Thanks," I said, and made my way to my regular table.

Dropping into a seat across from my fellow art geek, Tyler Thomas, I forced myself not to think about Lance and the other idiots.

***

I didn't see Todd or hear a peep from him the rest of the day, until art class. He slid into his seat just before the warning bell rang, exactly the way he'd done before when he didn't want to talk to me.

However, as soon as his butt hit the seat, he spoke.

"I'm not coming over after school."

Well, okay. Not that I was surprised, but that was pretty terse.

I nodded. "How come?"

"I'm just not."

I wouldn't ask again. I wasn't low enough to beg, and

really, what did I care? I could do the work myself. I didn't need him. He never had to show up again and the project would still get done.

That's what I'd wanted in the beginning, wasn't it?

But yeah, now the idea of it stung.

Miss Stockton began class, but her expressive voice and enthusiasm for the subject didn't lift my spirits like it normally did. Glancing away from Todd, I surveyed the concrete block wall that had been painted with bright colors and various scenes. Miss Stockton's first year, she'd assigned each of the art students one of the blocks to paint however we wanted, within reason of course. Mine was rose blossom, the flower not yet opened; it's potential not yet realized. I'd found the whole idea very poetic at the time. It did nothing to make my smile at the moment.

Instead, I moved my stare to the clock and willed the minutes to go faster.

It was the longest hour of my life.

***

Miller took off out of the school parking lot without so much as looking at any of his friends. No fist-bumps, no see-ya-laters. Nothing. And he took a left out of the parking lot, the opposite direction of his house. And yes, I knew that because I'd looked up his address.

Refusing to think about my reasons, I took a left myself, staying several car lengths behind him.

Winding through Sky Cove, winter hung in the air and the trees like some sort of morbid decoration. My mind raced with possibilities for Miller's actions. As much as I wanted to believe he had a legitimate reason for blowing off working on the project today, the part of me that refused to forget what he'd been like before we were assigned to work together screamed that he was just being a jerk.

I'd almost convinced myself that he'd returned to his selfish ways when he pulled into the Hospital Annex. The white brick building was one of several additions to the medical center, and it's crisp newness stood in stark contrast to the aging hospital. Turning into the adjacent parking lot, I watched as he climbed out of his truck, just as a woman stepped out of a silver Lincoln. Had to be his mom, judging by the obvious age difference and the fact that he hugged her.

Unlike Todd, his mother's hair was red, and she was short and small-framed. He must've gotten his coloring and build from his dad.

All my anger flew out the window as Todd walked with his mother into a door labeled *oncology*.

CHAPTER 13

Art class the following day was pretty much a repeat performance. Except that Todd didn't tell me he wasn't coming over after school. Instead, he just said nothing.

But he took off without a word as soon as the bell rang, just like he'd done yesterday.

I'd wondered about him all day. And worried. If his mom had cancer, or even thought she might have cancer, it made sense that he'd be out of sorts. Add to that the craziness with my animal carvings, and I figured he probably never wanted to talk to me again.

But still, I cared enough to want to know what was going on and if he was okay. So I grabbed my backpack and pulled up my hood, determined to get the parking lot in time to follow him again. If nothing else, I could catch him somewhere away from school and promise not to carve any more animals.

I could at least give him that reassurance.

I reached the parking lot just in time to hear Lance say something about *scraping the bottom of the barrel* and see Todd turn around and punch him in the jaw.

Startled, I hung back behind a row of cars, hoping not to

be noticed. I figured Lance's comment had something to do with me. God knew I didn't want to become the center of attention.

Although, with Todd's chilly silence as he threw the second punch, a nuclear bomb could probably go off and no one would notice. They were too busy watching.

Lance didn't really stand a chance against a much bigger, angrier Todd, but that didn't stop him from trying to hit back. His attempt just landed him on his butt when Todd grabbed his arm and shoved.

I held my breath, hoping Lance had the good sense to just stand up and walk away, preferably keeping his mouth shut.

But before he even got up from the freezing blacktop, Todd turned around, his eyes immediately finding mine, as if he knew I was there all along.

He stalked over to the where I stood, maneuvering his big body between two cars and coming to a stop right in front of me. I figured the crowd that had been so riveted by the fight was now watching the two of us with the same rapt attention.

"Can I come over?" he asked, anger barely coiled beneath the soft whisper of his voice.

"Of course." How could I say no when he clearly needed someone to unload on?

"I'll meet you there."

And then he headed off to his truck.

With a glance toward the crowd, I turned the opposite direction and walked to my car, hoping that speculation ended without rumor.

***

The ten-minute drive to my house seemed to take an eternity. I could see Todd a few car lengths behind me and hoped, for his sake, that no one else was following to see where he went. Speaking to me in the parking lot was risky enough without the high school hierarchy knowing he came to my house willingly.

I slowed as I approached Cliffhaven Lane, and as a turned on my left turn blinker, I noticed a truck pulled to the side of the road just beyond my turn-off. It looked eerily similar to another truck, though I couldn't be sure, because it had been totally dark when I'd seen a similar truck in front of my house the other night.

The hairs on the back of my neck stood up, as I parked in front of my house.

Todd pulled in right behind my car and was at the driver's side by the time I got out.

"I didn't know where else to go or who to talk to," he said, reaching behind me to push my door shut, eyes aiming at the slushy snow on the driveway the entire time.

I thought back to the oncology clinic the day before. Yeah, he had a boatload of stuff on his mind.

"Let's walk," I suggested, more than a bit unnerved by the sight of that truck.

There'd been a slight break in the weather, which in January meant that it wasn't Kelvin-level sub-zero cold. Today's temp was mid-thirties, and for a Maine winter it might as well have been a heat wave. Still, I zipped my heavy coat up over my hoodie.

"Your dad home?" he asked.

I shook my head. "I just figured you've got a lot to talk about, and it seemed like too big a conversation to have inside."

He shrugged. "Probably"

We took off down the drive and turned right onto the street. A wooded area near the curve would be a secluded enough place to talk.

We walked in silence for a few minutes, hoods pulled and hands stuffed in our jacket pockets, warding of the chill of the breeze.

"Lance just pushes my buttons, you know." Todd broke the silence as we neared the edge of the woods. "I'm so sick of him always thinking he's better than everyone else."

"No argument," I said. "But that attitude's nothing new with him."

"I guess my attitude's the new one." He looked over at me, eyes soft with sincerity. "The one where I've stopped treating people like shit for no reason."

"I've noticed that." It was remarkable really, the difference that had happened in him this school year. I knew I'd given him grief over what happened with Tina, and thinking of it just now still stung, but the truth was he'd been looking down his nose a lot less in the past few weeks.

We stepped off the road and into the trees, shoes crunching on unmelted snow and twigs and leaves. Stopping about twenty yards in, I turned to look at him. The woodsy smell of his soap was faint, but I caught a hint of it as the breeze moved between us.

"Does your change of attitude have anything to do with your mom?"

His eyes narrowed, and I could tell he wondered how I knew.

"I followed you when you left school yesterday," I admitted, figuring honesty was probably the best choice here. "I wasn't mad at you for not wanting to come over. I even expected it. I guess I just wanted to prove to myself that you had a reason for not coming, other than just flaking out on me."

"You saw where we went."

I nodded. "Then I thought back to that day when your mom called while you were at my house. You were so concerned, and yet there was such affection in your voice when you talked to her."

"She's got to have a biopsy," he said, a huge sigh escaping with the words, as if he'd been holding that breath all day long. "They think she might have breast cancer."

"Todd." It was all I could say past the lump in my throat. Instead of trying for some words of wisdom that would be empty and meaningless, I just took his hand in mine and squeezed.

"She went for her check-up back in the fall, and they did that test where they look for tumors."

"Mammogram."

"Yeah, that." He gripped my hand tighter. "They found a small lump, but weren't sure what it was. So she had another mammogram. When she called me the other day it was to tell me when she was going back in to discuss the results with the doctor. I told her I wanted to go with her."

"That was yesterday?"

He nodded. "The lump is bigger than it was when they first saw it, so they're going to go in and take it out, test it to see if it's cancer."

"Maybe it won't be."

"God I hope not."

He paced a few steps away, then turned and paced back, tension coiled tightly under his skin.

"Your mom's pretty special, huh?" Maybe if I could get him talking about her, the stress would ease off a bit.

"Yeah, she is. She's..." he stopped, as if he didn't know exactly how to put it. "She's good to me, always."

"You're lucky to have her."

"And you're lucky to have a dad who's good to you."

I thought back to the Facebook chat when he'd talked a bit about his father being pissed because he'd decided not to play basketball. Their relationship must be pretty strained.

"My mom's the only real parent I've got. My dad's just concerned with himself all the time. I'm pretty sure the only reason they stay together is because of me."

"I can't decide if that sucks, or if it's a good thing that they want to keep your family together."

"Far as I'm concerned it sucks," he said, leaning against a tree a few feet away, the tree limbs creating shadows on his face. "I've heard them arguing. I've seen how he treats her. Believe me, he's not setting a good example staying with her just because of me."

No wonder he'd been such a jerk to people.

"They had to get married. Or that's what they called it back then. Mom got pregnant right before high school graduation."

My heart ached for what he'd lived with, what he was now living through with his mom's potential health crisis. What would happen if his mom didn't make it? He'd be left with a father who didn't seem to care about anyone but himself.

And these were probably the exact questions he'd been asking himself since the cancer scare began. It would do no good to keep rehashing them.

"I'm so sorry," I said, at a loss for anything truly profound to say. Besides, it was the truth. I was terribly sorry for his family situation.

He shook his head. "It's not your fault."

"I know that, but I can still be sorry that you're living through it."

He pushed away from the tree he'd been leaning against and walked to where I stood. When he stopped, the toes of his boots nearly touched the toes of my tennis shoes and in the cold air I could see the breath streaming from between his open lips.

"That's the nicest thing anyone's said to me in a long time." His words came out on a soft whisper, not because there was anyone around to overhear, but because of the sincerity with which he said them.

I looked up into his eyes, the blue even brighter than usual as he fixed his gaze on me. What a conundrum he was, Mr. Popularity and all-about-appearances, and yet a kind, caring son and surprisingly nice friend.

And a really good kisser.

As if he read my thoughts, his eyebrows raised and he reached for my hands, pulling me closer until I bumped against him. His head titled to one side, and those blue eyes never left mine as he lowered his head.

There were all kinds of reasons that this was a bad idea, but as his lips touched mine, warm and welcoming in the chilly afternoon air, I decided I'd put off thinking about them. Instead, I wrapped my arms around him and just forgot about the rest of the world.

His mouth moved over mine with such intensity, such *possession* that I lost my breath. Kissing him in the woods, in the cold, winter air, after he'd just shared possibly the most difficult things in his life, well, I had no words for how perfect it felt.

Too perfect.

It seemed like forever before we pulled apart, and when we did it was only a millimeter. Our breath still mingled, warm and tingly between us. His arms tightened around my waist, and though it didn't seem possible, he pulled me even closer.

"I really, really like who you are," he whispered, eyes locked on mine, lips upturned in the slightest of smiles. "Really."

I started to smile back, but the lump in my throat stopped me, and sent tears blurring my eyes instead. When one spilled out and rolled down my cheek, Todd looked concerned.

I stopped whatever comment he was about to make with a shake of my head.

"Thank you," I said, my voice trembling. "I never thought it would, but it matters to me what you think."

Then his lips were on mine again and I found myself lost in the heat and fervor he seemed to generate in me. His hands found my face, simultaneously gentle and firm as he let his palms slide against my cheeks, his fingers working their way into my hair. Beneath the heavy winter coat, goosebumps rose all over my skin. My pulse hammered in my veins. But scarier than all that was the sweet ache that settled in my chest and the feeling of beauty that swamped my being.

I couldn't let this continue.

I broke the kiss, forcing myself to pull back despite the fact that every cell in my body was screaming for me to continue. If it was this hard to break away from him now, I could only imagine who awful it would be later on.

All the more reason to put a stop to this while I still had a chance.

But first, he deserved the truth from me.

"I really like who you are, too." I sent him possibly the most genuine smile of my life, because I meant those words from the depths of my soul. Todd Miller was nothing like he'd been in previous years, nothing like he portrayed to the world. But changing your image was near impossible in high school. He would never be allowed to jump off the popularity ship. Not without enormous consequences.

"But please don't kiss me again," I said, pain lancing my heart, leaving a gaping wound in its wake. "We can't do this."

I'd hurt him. The stunned look on his face told me that. But it also told me he hadn't thought this through. He hadn't considered anything beyond this moment, hadn't realized what the ramifications of these actions could be.

"What are you going to do, Todd?" I asked in a whisper. "Walk into school tomorrow holding my hand? Let me wear your football sweatshirt?"

I watched as he imagined those scenarios and knew he was seeing the same disaster I'd already imagined.

"The kids in your circles will never accept this. And by *this,* I mean *me.*"

"Maybe I don't care," he said, his voice brimming with the uncertainty I knew he felt.

"Yes you do." I placed my hand on his chest, felt his heart hammering even through the thick layer of his coat, and quickly drew it away. I couldn't touch him if I wanted to continue speaking. "And I don't blame you. High school's hard enough under the best of circumstances. It's even worse if you don't have a group of people to connect to."

"The fact that you know that first hand makes me so damn mad."

Sweet, so sweet that he was now my sort-of champion.

But so misguided.

"Ask yourself this," I said. "How exactly would this go over at school? With your friends? What do you think would happen if we walked into The Pizza Place together Friday night?"

I walked a few feet away, facing the other direction. I didn't want him to see my face and know how desperately I wanted him to say that he didn't care. That everyone else could just shove their opinions. That he wanted to be with me, really be with me, regardless of the fallout. It surprised me how very much I wanted him to say those words.

"I guess I figured nobody needed to know," he said.

And my heart broke in two.

Not that I hadn't expected that he wouldn't want the general public at Sky Cove Senior High to know he liked me, but hearing it was pretty brutal.

"It's not like any of them deserve to know anything about our business," he went on.

I had to agree on that point, but the fact still remained that he couldn't... *wouldn't* chose me. Not really.

"You're right," I said, turning to face him. "They don't. But I deserve not to have to hide. I've hidden from them for years, and maybe that's been a survival tactic for me. But I deserve to not have to hide anything else from them."

He stared at me, and I saw the conflict playing across his face. He was hiding himself, too. Hiding the man he was becoming because it didn't fit with the Sky Cove elite frame of mind. His attempt to break out by taking art instead of weight lifting hadn't been enough to sever the ties, but dating me would. And as I watched his face, I saw the moment he decided that he just couldn't take that step.

I wasn't mad. I understood.

But my heart splintered the rest of the way in pieces.

Unwilling to reveal to him just how much hurt I felt, I changed the subject quickly.

"We have to focus on finishing the project anyway." I started walking for the edge of the wooded area, heard his footsteps behind me. "Not to mention the business with my carved animals."

Thankfully, Todd took the hint. "Where do we even begin figuring out what the hell's going on with that?"

"No idea," I said as we stepped out onto the road and turned toward my house. "But for today let's just make some headway with the big project, then we'll talk about the other tomorrow."

Sounded practical enough, but the truth was I couldn't handle any more raw emotions right at the moment.

"And in the meantime you won't carve anymore animals?"

The hint of laughter in his voice told me we'd returned to at least a bit of the ease that had been between us... and reminded me exactly what I couldn't have.

My house now in sight, I mentally rattled off the tools I'd need for today's work, putting the project in the forefront of my mind, not allowing myself to wallow. I could do that later. For now, I was all business.

"Promise."

CHAPTER 14

"I can't believe how much you've done since the last time I was here." Todd looked at the completed carving of the rocky shoreline. "You'd barely started on that the other day."

I shrugged. "I was worried about you and your mom yesterday, so I put my worry to good use."

He sort of half-smiled, and I knew it was his way of thanking me for my concern.

"Let's go ahead and attach the shoreline to the main piece," I said assembling the necessary tools for the job. "That's the biggest part of the sculpture. I'll work on the hillside over the weekend, and after that, we'll only have the smaller pieces, like the houses and sailboats, to finish carving and attaching next week."

"Not much I can do to help with the carving," he replied, holding the sculpture steady as I mounted the shoreline with super-strength wood glue.

"It's okay." I held the pieces stationary once the glue was in place, giving it plenty of time to stick. "I'll put you on sanding or clean up duty."

Todd laughed and the sound of it slid over me, a lightness settling in my chest. His happiness somehow made me happy. And yeah, I refused to examine the reasons or implications of that.

"How'd you lose your mom?" he asked a moment later.

"Car wreck." I wasn't sure if it was a good idea to talk about how my mom died when his mom was facing a potential health crisis, but I figured he was working through all the possibilities in his head. "I was seven."

"Damn."

"Yeah. It sucked."

"You weren't living here then."

He knew this, of course. Most of the kids in Sky Cove had known each other forever, so it was more than a little obvious when I'd moved in during fourth grade.

"We were in Massachusetts," I answered. "Brockton. My mom was an accountant. Dad said he wanted to move out of the city so I could grow up in a safe place, but I think he just needed a fresh start. Somewhere without all the memories."

"Makes sense."

I nodded. "Moving here helped us both move on."

I decided to leave it at that and not mention how no one ever accepted me and making friends had been nearly impossible. And I was definitely not mentioning the fact that two years after moving here, I'd been the first girl in the sixth grade to develop breasts, leading to all manner of lewd comments from boys who were obsessed with boobs.

And people wondered why I wore baggy clothes.

Thankfully, Todd let the subject drop and we got back to the sculpture.

Finishing our work for the day, Todd grabbed his jacket and car keys preparing to head home. But instead of walking out, he turned back and sat down in the chair next to me.

"I can't leave until we talk about the animal carvings," he said.

"I won't do anymore. I promise."

He shifted closer, his nearness warm and welcoming, two things I did *not* need to feel.

"I don't want you to give up on the idea of entering that project in the scholarship competition."

"I can enter something else." I rolled my chair away,

pretending to dig around in my desk drawer. For lack of anything better to do, I pulled out some pictures of previous carvings I'd done. "See, I've got lots of things."

"But you planned this one for the competition." He scooted his chair, getting way too close again. "And I don't want you to quit."

"Well I'm not going to just keep carving animals when it causes you all kinds of problems!" With nowhere left to roll my chair, I stood up and walked toward the door. "I'm not that mean or vindictive."

"I know you're not." Todd stood as well, shrugging into his coat and palming his keys. "How many animals did you have in mind for the finished product?"

"I hadn't really finalized any plans, especially once the visions started wreaking havoc, but originally I'd thought about four of five."

"Well, you have three. So if you do one more, you can go ahead and complete what you originally wanted to do."

"But that means you'll shift again." I stared at the scuffed wood floor, my voice a faint whisper. The conversation was completely absurd. This situation was all kinds of crazy. But the only thing going through my mind at the moment was that I didn't want Todd to have to suffer through another shift.

"Yeah," he said. "It's okay."

"No, it's not!" I pushed away from the wall where I'd been leaning, intent on talking some sense into him.

"Just listen," he said, cutting off my protest. "What if you carve while we're together somewhere? That way it won't take me by surprise. I'll be prepared."

His words hit me like a punch in the gut, stealing my breath and quickening my pulse. In all my life, no one but my parents had ever sacrificed anything for me. And yet here was Todd Miller, willing to go through something horrifically painful and frightening just so I could finish a stupid project.

"No, Todd," I said, shaking my head. "I won't put you through that again."

"Phoebe, I want to do this." Hands settling on my shoulders, he squeezed gently but didn't pull me closer. "I want you to finish that piece for the competition, and I want to shift in front of you. Maybe it will give us some answers. Or at least reassure us that we aren't just losing our minds."

How he could be so logical about this astounded me. I was all set to abandon the project altogether, rather than cause him any more grief. But I had to admit, what he said made sense.

"I'll admit you have a point," I relented. "But I just can't imagine doing that to you again. And on purpose."

"Let's just think about it," he suggested. "I'll try to come up with a plan, and a place that would work. We'll talk about it again in a few days."

"Okay." Being this close to him, having him touch me, was just torture. In the interest of ending the torture, I nodded my agreement. "I'll try to come up with a way to make a sound that will stop it."

"Good idea."

He stepped away, his hands leaving my shoulders. The relief I felt was empty, leaving a dull ache in my chest.

I followed him out of the studio and to the back door, careful to keep my distance.

Hand on the doorknob, he turned back to face me. The smoldering in his eyes told me that he wanted to kiss me again, and I couldn't deny that I wanted exactly that. But he didn't make a move, and I knew he was honoring my wishes.

I smiled, hoping it conveyed at least part of the genuine emotion I felt.

With a quick nod, he was out the door. The click of the door latching behind him echoed painfully in my heart.

His truck rumbled to life outside in the driveway, as I went to the fridge to see what leftovers could be reheated for dinner.

And tried not to think about the feelings clogging my throat.

CHAPTER 15

I slept fitfully and woke up cranky. Good thing it was Saturday.

Weekends were nice because Dad and I actually got to spend whole days together, and I vowed not to let my current drama interfere with our family time.

As usual, I was up before him. Saturdays were his "sleep in" mornings, since during the week he got up earlier than he otherwise would in order to have breakfast with me.

I decided to fix the two of us a big breakfast this morning. The work would be a nice distraction from thoughts of Todd, magical carvings, and uncontrolled shape-shifting.

Twenty minutes later, the smell of coffee and the sound of sizzling bacon had my dad emerging from his bedroom. I smiled when I saw him. Unstylish jeans, a worn-out tee shirt from a mini-vacation to Lake Placid five years ago, and a rumpled head of hair that would probably still look the same at five o'clock this afternoon. That he was familiar and predictable soothed me.

"Morning, Dad."

"Hey there." He took a mug from the cabinet and poured

his first cup. "This is a treat."

"Just tired of cereal, I guess."

"No complaints."

I slid the last of the bacon onto a paper-towel lined plate and set it in the center of the table next to a bowl of scrambled eggs and a platter of toast.

"Dig in", I said, the table already set with plates and utensils.

For several minutes we ate in silence. It felt good. Natural. Then Dad had to go and ruin it by asking about Todd.

"How are things with the Miller boy?"

"Fine." I spit the word out quickly, to avoid groaning.

Dad raised his eyebrows. "Really?"

Of course he would know something was off. But I could not go into the complications of my relationship with Miller.

"Yes, Dad. Things are fine."

"What exactly does *fine* mean?" Dad asked, reaching for another slice of bacon. "Fine as in he's a nice boy, or fine as in he's awful and you just don't want to tell me."

I sighed. Dad wasn't going to give up.

"Neither, really," I answered. "He's not awful, but working with someone, especially someone I haven't ever really been around before, is just awkward and uncomfortable."

It was also uncomfortable to work with someone I was so attracted to, but I wasn't going there. I crunched into a salty bite of bacon and considered what to say next.

"I'll just be glad with this ordeal is over." That, at least, was the absolute truth.

"I know I warned you about that kid and his lazy reputation, but you realize there's more to people than you see on the surface, right?"

I stared at the burgundy tablecloth and nodded. He had no idea just how much I was aware.

"Well," he said, finishing off his coffee and the last of his eggs. "You're a good judge of character. I figure if you've spent some time with this boy, you've got a handle on him."

I resisted the urge to scoff out loud. Todd, I sort of understood. Myself, not so much.

I pasted a smile I did not feel on my face and looked up at Dad. "It's all good. Really. The gallery show's in three weeks and then life returns to normal."

Provided we figure out how to put an end to the shape-shifting issue.

***

Later that night, with Dad settled in his brown leather recliner with the newspaper and the evening news, I went to work in my studio. For a while I carved on the hillside that would mount to the right side of our sculpture, letting the small details of the work calm me. As usual, doing something creative gave me a bit of needed perspective.

We needed to be practical in our approach to my animal carvings leading to Todd's uncontrolled shape-shifting. As totally implausible as these events seemed, there had to be something out there to help us. Surely to goodness, in all of human history, there was someone somewhere who'd had similar experiences.

And like all of history, descriptions of such events would've been recorded or handed down in some kind or oral tradition. Perhaps there was a legend or folktale that could shed some light. After all, most legends began with a seed of truth that wound up exaggerated over time.

Putting away my caving tools, I laid the piece of the hillside on the long work table, then rolled my chair over to my computer desk. The internet meant the world was at my fingertips, and if someone somewhere knew something, I was darn well going to find out.

Two hours later, my enthusiasm waned and my neck ached from staring at the screen as I clicked on yet another link leading to a useless blog with some weirdo's list of reasons that we were all paranormal shape-shifters without our knowledge. I guess I didn't have any reason to be calling someone else a weirdo, but seriously. If I believed everything I'd read tonight I'd be aluminum-foiling the windows and sprinkling salt around the house to ward off the attacks from the aliens, zombies, vampires, and ghosts that roamed freely in search of innocent victims.

And good grief. If the government ever got a hold of these Google searches, they'd lock me up in the loony bin for sure.

I held out no hope as I clicked a link titled "Open Discussion Forum for the Otherworldly". In fact, I drummed my fingers against my desk out of boredom while I waited for the page to load. When the black background and purple letting began to come into focus, I imagined all the lunacy I'd likely be reading.

At first, the Otherworldly Forums seemed just like all the other crazy websites. Scanning the discussion titles, I found things like "Is it painful to grow fangs?" and "Can I counteract the effects of a full moon?"

I rolled my eyes.

But then a discussion near the bottom of the page caught my eye. "Does skinwalking still exist?"

Skinwalking? Sounded similar enough to shape-shifting. And the title of the discussion wasn't totally off-putting.

I clicked.

And sat stunned as I read.

I've read stories about skinwalkers. People who change into animal form spontaneously or because of some outside force. They can't control it. The stories I've come across all deal with stuff that happened centuries ago. Just wondering if anyone has any idea if such a phenomenon still exists.

Sounded eerily close to what was happening to Todd, minus the part about me having control of when he shifted or didn't shift. There were no other messages in the discussion, so before I lost her nerve, I hit the button to reply. At least this way it wouldn't drop off the front page and be forgotten forever.

Great. I needed a screen name and password. A few more clicks and a little typing, I was set to post as *Blondie17*. Stupid, I knew, but it was so far from anything I would pick for myself under normal circumstances, and I wanted nothing to even remotely tie me to anything I said here.

I tried for a nonchalant tone as I typed my reply.

Sounds like an interesting topic. I hope someone here has some information. Would love to look into this more.

I hit *reply* and closed out the page quickly, ordering myself to not sit there all night watching for someone to post another message.

Reaching for my phone, I flipped it open and searched for Todd's contact. Then I stopped.

No, I shouldn't text him. If I wanted to maintain any kind of emotional distance, I couldn't start texting him or Facebooking with him over every little detail. Besides, I had nothing earth-shattering to share.

And if I did, it could wait until Monday.

CHAPTER 16

The nasty cold returned on Monday morning, so much so that I dreaded the walk from my car to the school. Before opening my door and venturing out into the Arctic blast, I cinched the drawstring around the hood of my sweatshirt, pulling the hood tight around my face. I did the same with the hood from my coat, grabbed my backpack from the passenger seat, and took a deep breath.

I'd taken two steps when I heard the commotion from two rows over. A car door slammed and someone shouted. Glancing that direction, I noticed the meatheads Shane and Collin backing away from Todd's car, and Lance practically sprinting to the door of the school.

I said a quick prayer that Todd hadn't gotten into another fight and turned back in the direction of his car.

Todd stood, unmoving, by the hood of his truck. Okay, so at least he wasn't punching anybody. A larger red truck was stopped, though still running, right in the middle of the lane where students couldn't drive through and get to their parking spots.

"I can't believe you followed me to school," Todd said, his voice a weird mixture of fury and calm, which made no sense, but it was clear that he was holding back whatever anger he wanted to let loose.

"It's the only time I can catch you!" The shout came from someone I didn't recognize.

I knew immediately this was not a student. The voice was deep and gravelly, and really really pissed off.

Todd said nothing.

"You don't speak to me before you leave for school, and you avoid me all evening at home."

"It's not that hard to avoid you," Todd tossed back. "You're never home anyway."

Ah, his Dad. Which made sense. Big truck with a toolbox across the bed. Exactly the type of thing a contractor would drive. And yeah, the man in the heavy brown coat and black ball cap was not a happy camper.

No wonder the meatheads had run off.

Which begged the question, what in the world was I still doing standing around shivering in the wind?

"Look son, I talked to Coach Peterson. He said you can still be on the team even though you missed conditioning and try-outs."

"No." Todd's answer was quick and definite.

"What's your problem these days? You're throwing away everything you've worked for!"

"I'm not throwing anything away." Todd said, remaining still as a statue. "I'm making my own way, deciding what's important to me, and getting rid of the things that aren't."

"And I guess I'm just not that important to you, is that it?"

With that, Todd pushed away from the hood of his car and stalked over to where his dad stood.

"This is not about you! Don't you get that? It's about me and what I want!"

"And you're so sure you have all the answers, aren't you? You teenagers think you know exactly what's best for you and just ignore your parents' advice!"

"No, I just ignore your advice!" Todd yelled. "Mom

wants me to be happy. All you care about is yourself! The only reason you pretend to care about me at all is because you think my success makes you look good. As if me playing on the basketball team is going to make you more money or something. I'm sick of living my life just to make you happy, because guess what? You're never happy anyway, no matter what I do! You've never given a damn about me, so why the hell would I keep jumping through hoops for you?"

Wow. My heart broke for the boy who'd never known the real, strong love of a father. And at the same time, I beamed with pride for the young man who was standing his ground, becoming his own person, choosing his own path.

What courage and strength it must take.

Not wanting to be seen, I crept quietly along the row where I parked. A group of kids from several lanes over were making their way to the building, and hopefully I could fall in behind them and go unnoticed.

I turned my head to keep my face out of the biting wind, and got my first good look at Todd's dad. He was built like Todd, broad shoulders, long legs. But it was his eyes that caught my attention. I couldn't tell what color they were, but they emanated menace. He wasn't looking at me, didn't even know I was there, but the hairs on the back of my neck stood up anyway.

Completely creeped out, I pushed through the cold and into the school building, trying to forget what I'd witnessed and how it had somehow quadrupled what I already felt for Todd Miller.

***

Halfway through my peanut butter and jelly sandwich, Tyler Thomas slid into the seat next to me, followed by the sophomore girl he'd been paired with in art. Her name was Amanda. I think.

"How goes it, Phoebe?" he asked, scooting the ugly orange chair closer to the table.

"Fine." I looked at Amanda. "What are you doing in the cafeteria now? Don't you have sophomore lunch?"

Tyler and I and the other senior art students had somehow wound up in lunch with the juniors, due to some sort of scheduling snafu. For most of us, it didn't really matter, since we only ever talked to each other.

"We've got a substitute in fourth period," she answered. "I told him I needed to go to my locker and to the restroom. He'll never notice if I don't come back."

"Probably true," I said.

"So, how are things with Miller," Tyler asked, tossing his head to the side. His hair was as blond as mine and forever falling across his left eye. "It as awful as it seems?"

I should've figured that was the reason for Tyler's sudden interest in my project. While we were sort of friends, it wasn't like we talked about stuff that mattered. I supposed Tyler felt bolder due to the cute sophomore girl who now followed him around as if he hung the moon.

"It's not so bad," I said, glad that I could at least tell the truth about that. "He lets me call the shots and helps out where he can."

"He helps?" Tyler seemed surprised by this. "I figured he'd make you do all the work and just take half the credit."

"That's what I thought at first, too." I felt a bit guilty, remembering how I'd thought the worst of him when this project began, how I'd believed him to be shallow and selfish. It seemed like such a long time ago. "But he surprised me."

"I bet he still acts like a jerk, doesn't he?" This from Amanda, who for all I could tell had never really been around Todd at all. She'd probably gotten her information from Tyler.

The urge to defend Todd welled up in me, and I reminded myself not to be too overzealous. No need in making the situation any more difficult or awkward. But at the same time, I couldn't let people think he was walking all over me. Because he wasn't.

"Nah," I said, mustering as much nonchalance as I could. "He's been okay."

"Word is he's just in art because weight-lifting filled up," Tyler offered, opening up a bag of ranch flavored potato chips that smelled like someone's dirty gym socks.

"Well, whatever the reasons, working with him has been nothing like I thought it would be." That statement was the absolute truth and would hopefully put an end to all these questions. Too much speculation about the situation with Todd and me would just fan the flames of the high school rumor mill.

And the rumor mill was the last place I wanted to be.

Thankfully, Tyler took the hint and spent the rest of the time eating his lunch and chattering with Amanda. Left to my own thoughts, as I sipped on a bottle of orange juice, I tuned out the constant buzz of conversation in the cafeteria and thought back to what I'd witnessed in the parking lot that morning.

Todd's dad was an ass. And that was about the nicest word I could come up with. What kind of father confronts his son in the parking lot of school, in front of his peers, and yells at him over things that don't really matter?

Todd's strength and intelligence during the exchange still amazed me. And made me proud. It was almost as if their roles were reversed and Todd was the parent imparting wisdom to a fit-throwing child. And he was totally right. These were *his* choices, and had nothing whatsoever to do what his father.

That he was trying to break out of the superficial mold he'd been stuck in proved there was something genuine inside of him, something his mother had nurtured despite his father's ideas.

If his mom was sick, he'd be devastated. He would need a friend, someone who could understand him. Empathize.

My mom had been gone for more than ten years. Even now, there were moments when the loss felt raw and fresh. I didn't often let my mind replay those emotions, but knowing what Todd might be facing in the near future I couldn't help but remember.

If his mom had cancer, he'd need me. Because I could relate. And because he trust me.

Could I do that? Could I be the kind of friend he needed and still keep him at arms' length? Could I be there for him without letting our relationship go further?

Yes. Yes, I could. Because I have to. Because I wanted to.

If my heart got hurt in the process, I'd just deal with it later.

But there was something to be said for being smart, and I refused to make the eventual heartbreak any worse by starting something with him that could never go anywhere.

The bell rang, ending lunch period, startling me from the thoughts swirling in my head. Grabbing my backpack and tossing my trash in the garbage, I headed out of the cafeteria. I had one more class before art, which gave me time to figure out how to be kind without being inviting.

At least I hoped.

***

Art class was somewhat different, because all of the groups were working on their projects outside of class time. So, we worked on creating designs for posters to advertise our gallery opening. Todd and I worked together at our table, which gave me the chance to talk to him about what I'd seen in the parking lot that morning.

"Are you okay?" I asked, sketching letters onto the paper.

"Yeah," he answered. "Why wouldn't I be?"

"I saw you in the parking lot this morning." I kept my voice quiet and level, continuing to sketch. "With your dad."

"I was hoping you'd missed that." Todd grabbed a piece of paper and a pencil and began a drawing of his own. "Bad enough Shane and Collin saw it."

"And Lance," I said.

"Great," Todd groaned. "Like he needs some other

reason to give me grief."

"He didn't stick around long. He slithered off with Shane and Collin pretty quickly. Probably didn't want to get caught in the crossfire."

I continued experimenting with lettering styles, not looking at Todd. I figured it might make it easier for him to talk.

"How much did you see?"

"Enough." I cut my eyes toward his paper, noticing a pretty crude sketch of an artwork hanging on a wall. He wasn't much of an artist, but I smiled at his efforts. It made me happy to see him taking part in the creative process. "I thought you handled yourself remarkably well."

He shrugged and slid his drawing toward me. "You probably can't tell what this is, but I had an idea."

I let the subject change to our assignment. "Okay."

"Well, I was looking at the nice lettering you were drawing and thinking how pretty it is. It's like pretty enough to be artwork itself. And then I thought it would be neat if we did a poster within a poster."

"A poster within a poster?"

"Yeah," he said, pointing at his drawing. "Like this. You could draw it much better than me, but it would be a painting hanging on a wall, and you could make it look all fancy, like it was in an art gallery with people looking at it. But the artwork hanging on the wall would have your lettering on it, advertising our class projects."

For the first time, I looked at Todd as a creative person. Maybe he didn't have the drawing skills of someone who'd spent years developing the craft, but he'd had an idea. A vision. And that in itself was the spark of creativity at work.

It made me smile. It made me proud. It made me love him even more.

Love him?

All at once the air felt heavy and suffocating. That random thought, that one word that flitted into my consciousness without my consent, changed everything.

Suddenly, I saw the situation on a completely different canvas.

I *loved* Todd.

It was surprising. It was thrilling.

And I was scared as hell.

I must've sat there in stunned silence long enough to look weird, because Todd nudged me with his elbow.

"You okay?" he asked. "You zoned out there for a minute."

I shook my head, forcing thoughts of impossible love from my mind.

"Fine," I said. "Just picturing your idea. It's really good."

My approval seemed to please him, because he gave a half-grin and a shake of his head.

"So, Lance caught part of that crap with my dad?"

Yes, let's get back to that instead of me wallowing in newly discovered heartbreak. "Not much, but enough to get the drift," I answered. "But don't get in another fight with him. He's not worth it."

"I wouldn't fight over my dad anyway. He's the one who's not worth it."

"What did you and Lance fight over last week?" I asked. Although I'd heard Lance's comment about "scraping the bottom of the barrel", I really had no idea what had incited the fight.

"Lance is a dick," Todd said.

"That's common knowledge."

"He likes to cut people down, and I guess that day I was his target."

Clearly, Todd didn't want to tell me exactly what Lance had said, but for some reason I wanted to know. I wanted to know why, on that particular day of Lance being the ass he always was, Todd had hit him.

"What did he say to you?" I asked. "I didn't want to press you on it that day, because you had so much else on your mind."

"It's not important."

"It was important enough for you to hit him over."

"Phoebe, it was ugly." Todd whispered. "It was really ugly."

"Please." I stopped sketching and looked at him. "Tell me."

Todd sighed. He laid the pencil on the table and leaned closer. "He called me a pussy. And said I must really like trash because I was scraping the bottom of the barrel."

He was right. It was ugly. "I guess there's not much worse someone could call a guy in high school."

"I didn't hit him because he called me a pussy." He leaned further, until he was looking me in the eyes. "I hit him because he called you trash."

I couldn't breathe for the intensity in his gaze, the righteous indignation that was somehow, unbelievably for me. Clamping down on the love that now clamored inside me was a physical effort, the strain of it tensing every muscle in my body.

My pencil shook as I continued sketching, taking Todd's idea of the poster within a poster and adding my lettering.

After a moment, I felt safe enough to talk again.

"It's nice that you wanted to defend me, but it's really unnecessary," I said. "I've been dealing with worse than that for a long time. I'm immune to it."

Which wasn't exactly true. But I was *used* to it.

Todd shrugged. "It just kind of happened. I didn't even think. I just swung at him."

And naturally, if he'd taken a second to consider his actions, he wouldn't have hit him over a stupid comment about me.

"But I'm glad I did it." He slid his hand across the table, his fingers grazing mine softly, and my heart tumbled forcefully inside my chest.

I raised my head and looked straight into his eyes. All sorts of expressions played across his face. Gentleness. Friendship. Affection.

This was just not fair. I needed to be clear-headed,

objective. Not an airhead lovesick teenager.

Then Todd remembered we weren't alone and pulled his hand away, his eyes darting around the room to make sure no one had seen.

And just like that the moment was over.

I didn't fault him. After all, I'd been the one to highlight the list of reasons it would be a bad idea for the two of us to be involved beyond this art assignment.

But his actions still sliced my heart, just like I'd known they would.

CHAPTER 17

We mounted the hillside to the rest of the sculpture in relative silence, pressing and holding the piece until the glue had time to adhere. The project was looking more and more like I'd envisioned, and at least in that I could take comfort.

I was still so shaken by the conversation - and my revelation - during art class that I'd been even more "all business" than usual, gathering supplies and clipping out instructions to Todd with none of the normal pleasantries.

He didn't seem to mind. Maybe he was just as unnerved by his ill-thought-out hand grasp.

"It looks good," Todd said as we laid the project back in its resting spot on the worktable. "Cool that you can take a bunch of ordinary wood and turn it into something so pretty."

I smiled, but inside I felt weary and drained. I was finding it more and more difficult to navigate the emotional conflict of genuinely liking Todd - loving him, even - and wishing I didn't.

"Hey, listen," he began, dropping into one my chairs. "I was thinking about what we talked about the other day. You carving and me shifting in front of you."

I still didn't like the idea, but I knew he had a point. It might give us some kind of information that could possibly help us figure out what was happening and how to stop it.

"Wait a minute!" I said, rolling my chair over to my laptop. In the midst of talking about Todd's dad and Lance's ignorance, I'd forgotten all about the discussion forum I'd discovered. "I found something that might be a resource."

I'd memorized the website address, because no way was I bookmarking it. Todd scooted his chair closer to the computer screen.

"I searched online the other night," I started. "I ran across a bunch of nonsense that was no help at all, but then I found this place."

Todd watched with interest as the frilly purple font against he black webpage loaded. "Discussion Forum for the Otherworldly?" His voice sounded skeptical.

"I know. It sounds hokey. And some of it is. But there was this one discussion that sounded promising." I scrolled toward the bottom of the page. "Here it is."

I clicked. No new comments since I'd posted a reply, but at least it hadn't fallen off the first page yet.

"Skinwalking?" Todd studied the original post for a long moment. "I wish there was more information."

"Me too. I'm hoping someone will post some new information since I replied to the first post."

He pointed at the screen. "Blondie17 is you?"

I nodded.

"Seventeen is my football number," he said with a grin.

I'd known that, of course. "It's also how old I am."

"When's your birthday?"

Off the subject, but whatever. "April."

"You'll be eighteen then. You going to change your user name after that?" He was teasing, and darn it, it was cute.

"Hopefully by then I won't be posting on this site anymore."

"I hope you're right," he said. "But we should still go ahead with the planned shift."

"Planned shift?" I scoffed. "Sounds like we're going to work at the paper factory."

"Believe me, I'd rather."

"You don't have to do this," I replied. "I'd really rather not."

"I know both those things," he said. "But I want you to finish that scholarship entry and I need you to see me shift, so we have some idea what goes on when it happens."

"There's a possibility I won't see anything, Todd. When it's happened before, I see through your eyes. I see what you see."

He took in a deep breath, considering. "Even so, I still want to do it. There will surely be a moment, at least at the very beginning, when you'll see a small bit of the change. I mean, it's not a snap-your-fingers and it's done kind of switch. It takes a minute. And maybe you don't start seeing what I see until after the change is complete."

The ridiculousness of this conversation didn't go unnoticed.

"Okay." What else could I say?

"I think the hillside on the other side of the harbor will work," he said, pointing to the hillside on our carving. "There aren't any houses up there, and nobody goes up there in the winter."

"You're not talking about tonight, are you?" I was not eager to do this.

He shook his head. "I figure I'll watch the weather reports and try to pick a day that won't be too brutal."

Good plan. And I still had to come up with some way to stop the vision once it started.

"I should go," he said. "I want to be sure and be home before my dad, so he doesn't take his pissed off attitude out on Mom."

I swallowed hard. Of all the things I really liked about Todd Miller, his affection for his mother was possibly the most potent. I felt my eyes water.

"I'll cross my fingers you don't have any drama at your

house tonight," I whispered, careful not to let the emotion show in my tone of voice.

With a smoldering gaze and a smile that lasted a little too long to be comfortable, he grabbed his coat and headed out of my studio.

I didn't walk him to the door. And when I heard his truck pull out of the driveway, I did something I rarely ever did.

I cried.

CHAPTER 18

"What about a deer?" Todd asked, sweeping up the last of the wood shavings from the floor as I glued several small lean-tos on the hillside of our sculpture.

"I don't really think it would fit very well with the rest of the piece," I said, wondering why he thought we needed a deer on the hillside.

"Not for the project." He laughed, putting the broom back in the corner of my studio. "For your next carving. When I shift."

"Oh." I put away my carving tools, keeping my back to him. "I guess."

Honestly, the thought of doing this still really bothered me so I hadn't given it much thought. My feelings for Todd made it difficult to imagine the scenario objectively.

"I don't want to shift into something dangerous," he said. "Don't want to take a chance on hurting you."

I sat down at my laptop, thinking how impossible it was to maintain any sort of perspective when he said things like that. I typed the web address for the discussion forum, watching the various discussion topics load onto the screen until I felt able to respond without my emotions betraying me.

"I don't think you'd hurt me, regardless," I responded, still not looking at him. "If you're comfortable with that, it's fine."

"Just want to play it safe." He scooted a chair close to mine. "This weekend isn't supposed to be so frigid. What about Saturday night?"

I had no plans on Saturday night. I never did.

"What will you tell your parents?" I asked, turning away from the computer screen to look at him

"That I have a date." He smiled.

"Todd."

"What?"

"We aren't dating." As if I really wanted to point that out to him.

"Fine then." He slumped in his chair, resting his elbows on his knees. "I'll just tell them I'm going to hang out with some friends."

I turned back to the laptop, adrenaline bursting through me when I saw a new post in the skinwalking discussion.

"Hey, we got a hit."

Todd leaned even closer as I clicked the discussion. I could feel the heat from his breath on my shoulder as he eyed the screen with me. His nearness wreaked havoc on my resolve. I felt like my heart was somehow reaching for him... stretching and squeezing... creating a pain that radiated throughout my body. Everything in me wanted to turn my head and put my lips on his. It wouldn't take much, just a slight bit of movement, and then...

Finally! The page loaded. The post was from someone called *NightShader*.

I read out loud.

I've heard a little about skinwalking. I read somewhere about a curse where a man changes forms, but not on purpose. It's like it happens to him against his will. No idea on the details of how or why.

"A curse?" I said, trying to fit that piece of the puzzle into what we already had, which was next to nothing.

"Well, that gives us something," Todd replied.

"Another question."

"Instead of just shifting or skinwalking, now we can search for skinwalking *and* a curse."

He had a point. "Maybe it will narrow the results."

"I'll dig around, see if I can come up with a thread of useful info."

"Me too."

"Phoebe." He grabbed the arm of my chair and swiveled me to face him. "I think about you all the time," he whispered, his voice scratchy and laced with the same pain I felt.

He could not do this to me. He could *not*. "Todd, stop."

"I've tried to put aside what I feel, and I can't."

He reached toward me, taking my shaking hands in his.

"Don't." The shaking of my voice infuriated me as I realized I was on the verge of tears.

"I told you I wouldn't kiss you again, and I won't, as long as you don't want me to." He angled his head, forcing me to look at him. "I'm hoping you'll change your mind."

My heart swelled, tumbled around inside me, begging me to say yes. And part of me wanted to nod, to invite him back. It would be so easy. So good. I'd feel that warm rush of beauty I'd felt in the woods that day. His arms would be strong around me and for a moment I'd know what it felt like to be cherished.

For a moment.

Thoughts of the distance he kept between us at school flitted through my mind. He'd been careful not to sit too close after he accidentally touched me in art class a few days ago. Maybe he thought I didn't realize what he was doing. Maybe he thought I didn't care because it was me who'd told him we couldn't be a couple in public. Or maybe he'd thought I'd decide I could settle for these moments in private with him.

I wanted more than a moment.

If I couldn't have all of him, I didn't want any of him.

"Todd, no." My voice was nothing more than a whisper as I shook my head, swallowing hard against the lump in my throat. "Please."

He let go of my hands, his palms sliding away from mine with excruciating slowness.

"Okay," he said.

I turned my chair back to the computer as I heard him grab his keys and his coat. "I'll let you know if anything else pops up on this discussion."

CHAPTER 19

Saturday wasn't frigid, but late-January in Sky Cove, Maine was nowhere near balmy. So despite the above-freezing temp, I still bundled in my heavy parka and gloves and wound my scarf around my neck.

I'd told my dad I needed to get out of the house for a while, and that I'd just find a quiet spot to do some carving. All of which was true. It just wasn't the whole truth.

I wound my car up the hill until the gravel shoulder opened up wide enough to park my car. Todd had already arrived, and I could see the outline of his form in the driver's side of his truck. Reaching over to the passenger seat, I grabbed the tote bag that held my carving tools and stepped out into the chilly night air.

The sun dipped, not yet below the horizon, but low enough that only slivers of light slipped through the trees of the wooded hillside. It would give us enough light to find a decent spot for this experiment. The flecks of sunlight should've felt creepy, given what we were about to do, but I couldn't stop the stupid, girly part of me from thinking the half-light was somehow romantic.

Silently, I reprimanded myself for my moment of

weakness.

Todd walked toward me, a duffel bag slung over one shoulder. Beneath his coat he wore sweatpants that had seen better days, probably a decade ago. I figured attire didn't really matter.

After all, it's not like this was a date.

"I found a spot that's sort of a clearing," he said. "You mind walking a little?"

I shook my head.

My boots crunched the gravel and snow beneath my feet as we walked in silence. When we finally stepped off the gravel shoulder, I saw the small footpath that led into the woods. Good thing. I really didn't want to get lost in there.

Moving further into the trees, I felt a pang of familiarity, a crazy sense that somehow I'd done this before, walked this trail previously. Which was ludicrous. I'd never come up here before.

And then she was there, the woman from the vision. I hadn't thought of her. Hadn't imagined her. She just *appeared* in my mind, face still obscured, blonde hair still flowing about her shoulders. I knew she wasn't *really* there. I didn't see her with my eyes. And yet, she was more real than anything else in that moment.

I heard her voice then, the voice that I'd heard only once before but somehow knew like the back of my hand.

Her words were not an instruction, not a warning. They were a plea.

Please, may this be the last time we walk this path.

In my mind, I begged her to explain. Had she been a physical form, I would've grabbed on to her and refused to let go until she told me what was going on. As the image of her faded in my mind, her figure becoming translucent and disappearing gradually, somehow I knew she was the key to all that Todd and I were experiencing.

If I could just talk to her, ask her...

"Here it is." Todd stopped after about thirty yards at the edge of a small area of smooth ground. Stretched out between to groves of trees, the clearing offered enough space for a family picnic.

Or a couple of teenagers, one of whom might very well shape shift into a wild animal momentarily.

Unsettled by the vision, I watched Todd walk to the far side of the clearing, and unpack what looked like a change of clothes. First a red sweatshirt with his football number on the back, then a pair of black sweatpants that looked much nicer than the ones he had on. When he sat down and began untying his shoes, curiosity got the better of me.

"What are you doing?"

"Taking off my shoes."

Well, duh.

"Why?"

"So they won't tear up."

"Huh?" I asked, totally confused.

"My clothes don't make it through the shift," he said, nodding toward the clothes stacked on the ground. "That's why I wore old ones and brought a change."

"What happens to them?" I was completely flabbergasted. I had not even considered this. "Do they rip in two like the Incredible Hulk?"

"Um, no. I'm not exactly tripling in size when I shift into a fox," Todd laughed. "They sort of... I guess the best way to describe it is they disintegrate."

My eyes felt wide as saucers and I just knew my mouth was gaping open.

"So, when I start to shift back to my real self, you need to turn your back or close your eyes, unless you want to see everything."

My face heated and I was certain that my cheeks were now flaming red, but I managed to choke out, "Okay."

Shoving away the image of a naked Todd, I dropped down to sit on a fallen tree trunk, the bumpy log not exactly comfortable under my backside. I looked away from him and began unpacking my tools. I laid the small piece of wood, along with the gouge and the v-tool, on the ground in front of me.

When I looked up, Todd stood in front of me, looking down. He looked young. Innocent. Scared. So far from the over-confident, school jock I'd known before. I couldn't help but smile up at him.

I retrieved a scrap of paper with a picture of a small deer. I knew I could carve it from memory, but this potential shift was so important that I wanted to make it perfect. Todd's worry that he'd hurt me had been sweet, and though I thought it unwarranted, I wanted to reassure him.

Handing him the paper, I said, "I picked out a picture of a small deer. Didn't want you to worry about being dangerous or anything."

He nodded. "Thanks."

The wind picked up, creating a chill in the air and an ominous sound that reminded us why we'd trekked to this spot in the woods. Todd turned to walk back to the other side of the clearing. He stopped about halfway and turned back to me.

"What did you figure out about stopping the vision?"

Reaching into my bag, I pulled out the whistle attached to a lanyard and hung it around my neck. I held the whistle up for him to see, then popped it in my mouth.

He nodded, then headed across to the opposite side.

"Ready when you are," he called, leaned against a tree trunk.

I wasn't ready at all. I dreaded what I was about to do to him. I prayed it gave us some answers, because if I put him through this for nothing, I'd never be able to forgive myself.

Before I talked myself out of it, I grabbed the gouge and the chunk of wood and went to work. The sun that slithered between the trees moved lower as I worked, and I pushed myself to carve faster. I didn't want to be out here in the pitch black. The little deer began to come to life in my hands, and I switched to the v-tool for more detail.

As I gave attention to the tiny eyes, I heard Todd begin to move across the clearing. Cutting my eyes that direction for the briefest of moments, I saw the trembling in his legs. My heard sank and I fought the overwhelming urge to drop the carving right then and stop this from happening. But Todd had insisted on this, and for that reason alone I would see it through.

I dropped my eyes back to the carving, clenching my jaw to create a stronger hold on the whistle between my lips. As the eyes of the deer became clearer Todd's movement increased. He pushed away from the tree and moved to the center of the clearing, his steps uneven and his actions sporadic.

A moment later the eyes were complete and I looked up from the carving. Todd's gaze caught mine for a split second before his form began to blur.

The wind howled through the clearing, disturbing the leaves and twigs on the ground. In front of me Todd glowed, his body a bright white outline of a human, his distinguishing features obscured by the blinding light.

My heart pounded so hard I could feel the blood rushing through my veins as Todd's cry of pain rent the air. My stomach pitched violently and for a moment I was afraid I would be sick.

Of all the ways I had imagined this scenario would suck, I couldn't have dreamed how hearing him cry out in pain would crush me inside.

As my peripheral vision began to fade, narrowing in on the light in front of me, the Todd's lighted form began to shrink, change shape, and all at once the shouts stopped.

And for a split second, the form of a deer stood before me.

At once, sea of black nothingness obscured my sight, and I considered blowing the whistle and ending this right here

But the blackness was gone, and I wasn't looking at the deer anymore. I was looking at myself.

Sitting on the log, v-tool and carved deer in my hand, whistle stuck in my mouth, I looked exactly as I knew I must. And yet, I was somehow different.

Around me a soft light emanated, creating a halo effect. The green of my eyes sparkled, amplified by the light around me. The strings of hair that escaped my ponytail to fall haphazardly around my face looked like golden silk. My skin, the same fair white as always, looked more like fine porcelain.

I was beautiful.

How was the possible? How could I be exactly the same and yet be so beautiful?

This is how I see you.

The thought flew into my consciousness, bombarding me with meaning I refused to think about. This whole stupid experiment was about figuring out what the hell was going on, not about expounding on the feelings that existed between Todd and me that could mean nothing but heartache.

I saw you shift. I sent the thought in his direction bringing this impossible telepathic conversation back to the subject at hand.

Good. You okay? If he'd just quit worrying about me for a second, it would be so much easier.

Fine. Think it's okay to end this now?

Probably so.

I took one last moment to look at myself through Todd's eyes. In the second before I blew the whistle, I admitted to myself how badly I wished I could feel that beautiful.

But that was my weakness talking, and I wouldn't give into it.

Inhaling quickly, I forced my lungs to work and blew the whistle, which proved much more difficult than I anticipated.

And just like that I was back in my own head and Todd was a glowing ball of light again. As his shape began to change and expand, I heard his moans of pain start again. Part of me wanted to rush toward him, to somehow offer him comfort, and yet the sensible part of me knew there was nothing I could do, other than hope the shift back to his natural form was quicker.

Across the clearing, illuminated by the light pouring off Todd's form, stood the woman I'd seen in my visions, the woman whose voice had spoken to me on the walk here. Her face, still unclear to me, turned toward Todd, and from her I felt a sense of regret and deep longing.

Whatever was going on she seemed genuinely sorry that Todd was suffering.

When she turned from Todd, I saw the man standing next to her. I didn't recognize him, but the tunic and cloak he wore spoke of a time long ago, as did the woman's emerald green dress with long flowing sleeves. How any of this was possible I had no idea, but there was no denying the emotion that flowed between the two of them.

As the last of the light faded from around Todd and I saw the natural outline of his body, the woman and the man in the background also began to fade.

Bodies becoming translucent, the gap between them widened as they each reached a hand toward the other. No amount of reaching was enough, and they remained separated as they shimmered into nothingness.

But just before the last molecules disappeared, I heard him speak, his voice as lyrical as hers.

"I am so very sorry." His words rang out to her as the two of them vanished from sight.

I gasped, not realizing I'd been holding my breath. The whistle fell and dangled around my neck. I had no answers, no idea what the implications of what I'd just witnessed were, but I'd digest it all later.

Todd lay, face down, crumpled on the ground. And yes, as he'd warned, his clothes hadn't survived the shift.

Ignoring the emotions this event had stirred up in me, I ordered myself into action. It was cold outside and Todd was naked. I jumped from my seat on the log and dashed across the clearing to where he'd laid his clothes. Without looking – well, okay, maybe I did glance for a half-second at his butt – I dropped the clothes and his coat on top of him and sat down beside him, back turned.

I didn't know how long I sat there, Todd still motionless on the floor of the forest. It might've been an hour. It might've been sixty seconds. My mind was so full of images and feelings from what I'd just experienced that I couldn't focus on something as menial as the passage of time.

I didn't even register the cold temperature as the sun began to disappear from between the trees.

Lost deep in the memory of the woman and man I'd seen, I didn't notice Todd stirring behind me. The rustle of the leaves beneath him caught my attention the same time his hand reached up to touch my knee.

Instinct had me almost turning to look at him, acknowledge him, but I caught myself just in time.

"You didn't look, did you?"

His voice sounded weak, but I managed to catch the bit of humor lacing his words. He was worried I'd seen him naked.

"No more than I had to to throw your clothes on top of you." I laid my hand on his, gave it a gentle squeeze.

"What about before?" he asked, sounding weaker than before. "You saw me shift. Right?"

Without looking at him, I nodded my head. "But we can talk about it tomorrow. For now, let's just get home and get some rest. That had to be exhausting."

I felt him sit up, and I clenched my fists against the damn curiosity that had me wanting to turn my head.

"Okay," he said. I could tell by the sounds behind me that he was pulling the shirt over his head. "Just don't look."

CHAPTER 20

I slept until almost eleven o'clock the next morning, and for the first time in a long time, I woke without the immediate desire to get into the studio to create. The events of the night before had completely wrecked me, and despite a seemingly sound and dreamless sleep, fatigue still swamped my body.

I heard my dad in the living room flipping channels on the television. He probably wondered if I was sick, given that I never stayed in bed this long. Of course, I also never went out on Saturday night, so perhaps he thought my sleep-in had something to do with a social life.

He'd be so disappointed if he realized what this really was.

I grabbed my laptop from the nightstand, thankful that I'd thought to take it from my studio when I came home last night. Propping up against my pillows, I set the computer on my bright green comforter as I typed in the web address for the Otherworldly forum. I figured there was nothing new, but the chance existed that something else might've been posted. While the black and purple page loaded, I opened another tab and Googled "skinwalking curse". That there were over two million hits should not have surprised me, but I shook my head in disbelief anyway.

Saving the search results for later, I clicked back to the forum and scrolled until I found the discussion thread on skinwalking.

My breath caught when I saw three new posts.

The first one was written by *P_Browning_Ed.*

The skinwalking legend is most commonly found in Native American stories, but the origins of the concept are also found in European myths. Werewolves and lycanthropes are the most widespread stories that include humans turning into animals, but those are simply the ones our culture is most fascinated by. Skinwalking and curses that involve the shifting of humans into animal forms are as varied as the colors in a box of Crayolas.

I took half a second to recognize that the poster sounded like he was writing a doctoral dissertation, then went on to the next one, posted by *CallMeCrazy1999.*

I read up on skinwalking a few years ago. Previous poster is correct. Most of the info you find, especially online, deals with Native American legends – specifically Navajo. However, after some digging around, I found a little known story about a Druid priestess who cast a skinwalking spell. (Although I'm sure it wasn't called 'skinwalking' back then.) I never found much about how or why the curse was cast, but I thought it was interesting to find the idea of skinwalking pop up in Druid history.

Druids? Wizards or something like that from the Celtic regions, right? I opened a third tab on my browser, searched for the Wikipedia article on Druids. I was mostly right. Druids were some sort of ancient priestly class in the British Isles.

The third post came from *MiketheParanormalist.*

Never heard the Druid thing, but I have heard that skinwalking goes much further than Native American legends. Like way back to the beginnings of civilization. I read one story that said some skinwalking curses were multi-generational. Maybe it has something to do with family bloodlines.

Well, that was certainly some new information. Druids

and bloodlines and curses. Part of me wanted to laugh at the absurdity, but a bigger part felt pretty unnerved by the enormity of the situation Todd and I had found ourselves in.

I should tell him about the new posts. And we still needed to talk about what had happened last night. But the thought of seeing him...

My phone vibrated in my purse, pulsing against my keys with a ratchety sound. Reaching to the floor beside my bed, I grasped the strap and hauled it up onto the mattress.

It was a text. From Todd.

Can I come over?

I couldn't really say no. We needed to talk. The complexity of my feelings for him couldn't get in the way of dealing with this unexplainable craziness.

I texted back. *Just woke up. Give me an hour.*

If my emotions were going to be a wreck, at the very least I could take a shower and be somewhat put together physically.

***

"I didn't lose my own vision until you were completely shifted," I said, carving some small details on a tree for the hillside of the project. We'd decided to work while we talked, so while I carved, Todd sanded the long pieces that would eventually form the border of the sculpture. "Everything went black for a split second, and then the deer was there."

"So you saw me while I was changing?"

We kept our voices quiet, but the noise from the basketball game on the television pretty much assured that my dad was not listening. It felt strange, having Todd here while my dad was home. But Dad had been cool about it, and hadn't made a big deal.

"Sort of." I switched tools to work on the trunk of the tree. "You were surrounded by this bright ball of light, so I didn't exactly see *you*. But I saw the light shrink smaller, and then there you were. A deer."

And the bizarreness quotient just amped up even higher.

"Then you saw through my eyes?"

"Yes."

"And you saw yourself the way I see you," he said, his voice soft and warm and all the things I wished we could be to each other.

I did not want to discuss this. It was too personal. Too intimate. And far too dangerous.

"I guess that's a byproduct of the situation," I answered, trying and failing to make light of it. I changed the subject. "I've never asked you what *you* see when you shift."

He shrugged. "I see what I'd see otherwise. The trees, the plants. Whatever's there in that place, that's what I see. My eyes are just closer to the ground."

How crazy to think his six-foot one-inch linebacker body shrunk down into an animal the size of a fawn.

I switched subjects again. "What was really interesting was what I saw after I blew the whistle."

He stopped sanding and looked at me, his blue eyes narrowing. I could tell he was disappointed I'd switched subjects, but he didn't push it. After all, the way he saw me had very little to do with what we were trying to accomplish. His chair scraped across the wood floor as he scooted even closer.

"There was a woman, in a long, old-fashioned looking gown. And a man, also in really antiquey looking clothes."

"In the clearing with us?" His quick intake of breath indicated his surprise, and also his worry that someone might've seen what happened to him.

"Yes and no," I replied. "They were there, but not really."

He raised his eyebrows. "Explain?"

I took a deep breath, tried to ignore the clean scent of shampoo that clung to his still damp hair, and plowed forward. I figured nothing could sound any weirder than what we'd already experienced. "I guess the way to describe it is that they were in another dimension. No one else would've been able to see them."

"So why were you able to see them?"

"I think they wanted me to," I said. I'd thought about it all morning, and that was the only explanation. "I think they let me see them because they had something important to share."

"Did they say anything?"

"The man did. Just before they vanished."

"Well?" he asked.

"As soon as I blew the whistle, I was back on that log, seeing you through my own eyes." I shifted in my chair so I was looking at him and felt that same jolt I always felt when I saw him. Like some kind of electric shock straight to my heart. "The form of the deer was glowing, getting larger, and I could hear you moaning and struggling. It was agonizing. I couldn't see details of the woman's face, but I could see that she was watching you. And I could feel this sense of regret, and... aching from her. She was seriously saddened by what was happening."

"What about the man?"

"He reached out to her," I said, my mind playing the vision like scenes from a movie. "But the closer you got to returning to your normal self, the further apart they drifted. She lifted her arm to reach for him, too, but no matter what, they couldn't reach each other. And then the light from your form faded, and the man said something to her." Todd's eyes widened. "What?"

"He said, 'I am so very sorry.' And then the light was gone, they disappeared, and you dropped to the ground."

"What do you think he was sorry for?" he asked, his voice a breathy whisper. He'd been totally transfixed by the story.

"I'm not sure. And I don't know what she regretted either. But it had something to do with what was happening to you."

"So now we have a man, a woman, skinwalking, and a curse."

"And a Druid priestess," I added, figuring it was as good a time as any to show him the latest posts on the website.

"A what?"

Finished with the tree carving, I laid the small figure on the table and put my carving tool back into the pouch. Todd sanded the last of the border pieces and placed them on the table as well.

"There are new posts on the Otherwordly forum," I said, rolling my chair over to my desk. "Come see.

He picked his chair up and scooted closer so he could see my laptop screen. I immediately regretting inviting him to *come see*, as I could feel the heat from his body as he leaned over my shoulder. My gut clenched from the desire to lean back against him. To feel the strength of his chest and arms.

I hated myself for wanting something that could never be.

I scrolled down far enough so that Todd could read the posts. I didn't want to look at him, but as his eyes traveled back and forth across the screen I couldn't tear my own eyes away. So serious. So intense. A side of him I'd have never known had fate not thrown us together.

Another side of him I loved.

Good grief. Could my life get any more pathetic?

"You should post a reply," he said, eyes still glued to the screen.

"Why?" I looked away and pretended to be busy with the computer. "I don't think those people have any more information than they've already shared."

"Maybe not. But they might be able to tell us where they found their info. A website or a book or something. If we could look at it for ourselves, we might see something they didn't pick up on."

He had a valid point.

I logged in as Blondie17 and clicked to reply.

Wondering if any of you could tell me where to find this information. Did you find it all online or is there a book I could get my hands on? Would love to research this topic a bit further.

"There," I said, closing the laptop. "I'll keep a watch to see if anyone comments. And in the mean time, I'm not carving any more animals."

"I don't want your project to go unfinished," he said.

I stopped his argument with a raise of my hand. "Four animals is enough. I'll just focus on getting them displayed in a shadow box. Maybe do some decorative carving for the frame. It will be fine."

"You sure?" He angled his head and leaned closer.

Darn his concern for me. It warmed places inside me that should just stay cold.

"I'm sure," I said. "Our project for art class is almost done. All we need now is to assemble it."

"Tomorrow after school?" He seemed pleased that our assignment was coming together.

"We'll attach the small pieces and let them dry overnight. Then Tuesday we'll mount the border around the edges, and it will be done."

He took a deep breath. "I'll miss coming over here to work on it."

"Yeah, well," I stammered, at a total loss for words. My pulse raced and my skin heated, as I fought for control of my emotions.

"But we'll still have class together, not to mention all this business with the shifting. I guess we'll still see plenty of each other."

The fact that my heart smiled at that thought nearly made me choke.

Pulling myself together, I smiled at him and nodded. "I'll be around."

"I should go," he said. "Mom's expecting me home in time to help with dinner."

Long-tense muscles in my body relaxed at the knowledge that he would soon be gone. Too bad my heart couldn't be as glad.

"See you tomorrow," I said, occupying myself by straightening my desk.

"Bye Pheebs."

He pulled the door shut quietly and said a polite goodbye to my dad.

When I heard his truck crank in the driveway, I let out the breath I'd been holding.

Pheebs. He'd given me a nickname.

I smiled, inside and out.

And cried again.

CHAPTER 21

As planned, Todd and I began the finishing touches on our joint project on Tuesday afternoon. All small pieces had been attached with wood glue the day before – boats, trees, lean-tos, and clouds. I'd forgone the seagulls, though, for Todd's sake.

Carefully, and without talking, the two of us worked to attach the heavy border pieces that would frame the sculpture. Two clamps on the back of the project would hold a wire that would allow us to mount the sculpture on the wall.

After positioning, gluing, and holding the border pieces for what seemed like hours, we very gently propped it up against the wall to get our first good look at it.

I stepped back, putting a few feet between the piece and me. My breath caught in my throat and moisture collected in my eyes. Stunning. It was absolutely stunning.

I'd always had pride in my work, always looked at my creations with both an objective eye and a rush of pleasure. But never had anything I created taken my breath away.

Beside me I felt Todd lean closer. His arm came around my shoulder, and warmth from his body surrounded me. He didn't speak, but the squeeze of his hand told me he was proud of the finished product as well.

This wasn't just *my* work. I hadn't done this alone. Maybe the original idea had been my brainchild, and maybe my skills had been responsible for the life-like sailboats and houses. But everywhere I looked I saw traces of Todd.

In every figure that stood out in relief from the background, I saw the way he'd helped carefully attached it. In every tiny little nook-and-cranny detail that I'd carved, I saw the way he'd swept up the debris, never once complaining.

And when I looked at the final product, I saw a small piece of Sky Cove history that Todd and I now shared. I knew I would never think of the harbor again, never go there to sketch and to think, without thinking of him and the time we'd spent working together.

I realized then that I was going to miss him.

It was what I'd been afraid of all along.

"It's really beautiful," he whispered. "You did amazing work."

I shook my head, the lump in my throat keeping me silent.

"No really, I think it's great." He'd misinterpreted my reaction to his words.

"I didn't do it by myself," I said, not looking at him. I couldn't afford to let him see the tears gathering in the corners of my eyes. Couldn't let him read my expression.

I felt him shrug. "I didn't do much. You did all the creative stuff."

"You're still a part of it," I said. "And it's the best piece of art I've ever had a hand in creating."

I looked at him then. Big, stupid mistake. Huge, crazy mistake.

I'd told him never to kiss me again, and he'd done what I asked. He hadn't made a move since that day in the woods.

But I saw it in his eyes in that moment. The longing. The desire. The project that had brought us together was now finished. We were getting closer to discovering the truth about the skinwalkers and where the two of us fit in the legend.

There was just too much between us to deny it any longer. But because he'd promised, he wouldn't.

He held back.

I went up on my tip-toes and fixed my eyes on his. I watched as they widened, his pupils dilating as I slid my hands around his shoulders.

Knowing it was the most foolish, reckless moment of my life, I pressed my lips against his. And what I felt from him was so completely foreign.

Acceptance. Admiration. Belonging.

It was in the way his arms tightened around me as we kissed. It was in the way he moaned from deep in his throat. It was in the way his entire body screamed *finally*.

Somewhere along the way I'd stopped expecting the sneering mockery I normally received from my peers. I'd stopped bracing for insults or rejection.

Somewhere along the way I'd let him in. I'd let him see me. And instead of laughing and walking away, he'd stayed.

As the kiss slowed, Todd's hold increased around my waist, as if he was afraid that as soon as it ended I'd pull away.

He wasn't entirely wrong.

But as his lips left mine, he smiled down at me, pressed a kiss to my forehead, and pulled me even closer, resting his chin on top of my head.

His embrace wasn't forceful. I didn't feel like he was holding me against my will. Instead, I just felt secure, warm, content.

And, God, it was nice.

He didn't say anything for a long moment. It should've been uncomfortable, wondering what his reaction to the kiss would be. But it wasn't.

"What are you going to wear to the art show Saturday?"

Of all the things he might've said following that curl-your-toes kiss, I never would've imagined *that*.

"Huh?" Well, that was a brilliant response, but it was the best I could come up with.

"Are you going to dress up for the show?" he asked.

"I don't know why it matters," I said, clueless as to where this conversation was heading.

"It matters." He pulled back to look at me, pressed his lips to mine in a quick kiss. "It matters because your work is going to be the star of the show, and I want everyone to see that you're just as beautiful as your art."

My heart flipped, then thudded solidly in the soles of my feet. Where had Todd Miller learned to say such soul-melting things? Where was the Miller that had acted like a jerk toward everyone he considered beneath him?

I had a sinking suspicion that soul-melting Todd Miller was the real one, and had been lurking beneath the school-jock front all along.

I wanted to tell him that being the center of attention was not something I was prepared for, that I'd much rather blend into the background, but the look in his eyes was so genuine that I just couldn't do it.

"I guess I could find something nice to wear." I almost didn't believe the words came out of my mouth, but then Todd's arms tightened once more and he lowered his mouth to mine.

I guess by initiating the first kiss, I'd given him permission to keep on. And I couldn't find it in myself to regret it.

Nothing was settled between us. No mention of a relationship or public acknowledgement had been made. Maybe it didn't matter. Maybe what we felt for each other went beyond the traditional necessities of high school dating.

Maybe knowing he felt *something* for me mad sharing these moments in private enough.

In my mind I knew I was lying to myself. But my heart refused to accept it. And I was tired of fighting these feelings. So tired.

As his mouth moved over mine again, warm and unyielding, I decided that I deserved this. All of it.

I deserved the happiness that bubbled inside me when I was with him. I deserved the rush of emotion and pleasure that filled me when he touched me. And when it ended – and I knew it would – I'd deserve the heartbreak for allowing myself to give into these weaknesses.

But at that moment, I kissed him back with all I had, because this thing between us was fleeting, and I wanted to enjoy it while it lasted.

Regardless.

CHAPTER 22

Our art class showed up early on Saturday afternoon in order to decorate the school cafeteria for the art show. Our posters had been hanging on the hallway bulletin boards all week, advertising our event for the small handful of students who cared. Fliers had been mailed to local businesses and an ad placed in the weekly Sky Cove Gazette. I hoped someone other than all our parents would show up, but I wasn't going to hold my breath.

Todd pulled his truck into the school parking lot and slowed, not in a big hurry to find a spot. He'd surprised me by suggesting that he pick me up, but as he'd pointed out, we needed his truck to move the sculpture, and if I rode with him, my dad could drive me home when the show was over.

We ran late because it took a bit of extra effort to get the piece loaded in the bed of his truck and secured so it wouldn't slide around during the drive. The other cars in the lot were empty, the students all inside already.

I noticed Todd eyeing the empty cars and wondered if that had been his plan all along, to avoid being seen arriving together.

But then he tugged playfully on my ponytail, and I

decided not to worry about it.

"It's almost show time," he said with a mischievous smile, leaning across the seat. "I'm really proud of you."

And then he kissed me, quick and hot, and I forgot about whatever misgivings I'd been chewing on a moment ago.

He pulled the truck up to the side entrance of the cafeteria. "Go on in. I'll get a couple of the guys to help me unload it."

I nodded, too dazed by that kiss to argue. "Just be careful with it."

"No worries," he said with a wink.

***

The cafeteria was barely recognizable once the decorations were complete. Miss Stockton had transformed the place with a lovely elegance that was in no way stuffy or formal, but rather inviting and imaginative. Which was exactly the way she did everything.

The circular tables were draped with velvet tablecloths in alternating colors of burgundy and black, each displaying one student's smaller pieces of artwork. Tall, silver floor lamps spotlighted the works hanging on the wall. A long table near the back of the room contained punch and refreshments.

"Everything looks marvelous!" Miss Stockton proclaimed, circling around with her arms extended. She was nothing if not a bit dramatic. "Now go and get yourselves ready and be back in a half hour."

Todd stood beside me, our sculpture hanging on the wall. My smaller pieces were displayed on the table closest to it, and Todd's eyes narrowed as he studied them.

I'd finished the shadowbox animal display, which sat on a small easel in the center of the table. I'd also chosen a few of my drawings and framed them, including the sketch of the woman I'd done at the harbor a few weeks ago.

"Is that the woman from the clearing that night?" he asked.

"Yes." I'd wondered if he'd figure that out.

"When did you draw this?"

"Several weeks ago," I admitted. "I've seen her before. Heard her voice even."

"Why didn't you tell me?"

"I didn't know she had anything to do with what's going on with us."

"Do you normally have visions like that?" he asked. "Or hear voices?"

I shook my head. "I thought it was stress."

"What has she said to you?"

"Nothing that made much sense," I said. "Once I heard her say 'You choose to deny'. That was in art class not long after we came back from Christmas. Once, after I drew that picture, I felt like I was being drawn into it, like I could feel her sadness. Then the other night, while we were walking to the clearing, she said 'Please may this be the last time we walk this path.' And then, I saw her and the man when you were..." I looked around, noticed a few other students still in the cafeteria. "You know."

"A few more puzzle pieces," he said. "We'll try to put them all together later."

"Okay."

"Tonight," he went on, gesturing to the sculpture on the wall and my pieces on the table, "is all about you. Let's go get ready."

***

I did the best I could in the drab school bathroom. Not that I ever fooled much with my appearance. But as I surveyed myself in the small, cracked mirror, I decided I'd done pretty well.

In the back of my closet, I'd found a pair of black dress pants I'd worn to my aunt's funeral last year. A trip to the consignment shop the other day had yielded a really frilly, feminine, ivory see-through blouse with lacy bell-shaped sleeves and an ivory camisole beneath. I'd even splurged on a fancy hair clip decorated with pearls.

With my blond hair twisted and secured with the clip, I pulled a few strands to hang loose around my face the way I'd seen in magazines. I wasn't much on make-up, but I applied a bit of blush, some light mascara, and pink lip-gloss.

I looked completely foreign to myself, and yet, at the same time, I sort of liked it. I felt different, but not in a bad way. The green of my eyes seemed brighter, more pronounced. The shape of my face, which I'd never noticed before, appeared delicate.

I remembered seeing myself through Todd's eyes and wishing I could feel as pretty as I'd looked. Maybe what I felt now was somehow giving me an idea what that was like.

I hung my jeans, tee shirt, and hoodie on the hanger in my garment bag, grabbed my tote bag, and headed to my locker to store it all.

I saw him when I shut my locker. He'd crept up on me while I'd been stowing my things inside. Leaned against a locker a few feet away, he looked every bit the dashing gentleman. Black, flat-front slacks, dark purple button-down, and a satiny tie in the same shade.

Oh. My. Gosh.

I had to check to make sure my tongue wasn't hanging out of my mouth dripping drool down my chin.

I reached for the locker to balance myself. It would be just like me to stumble at a moment like this, and given I was wearing strappy black heels – also from the consignment shop – falling over from a massive hormone rush was a distinct possibility.

"Wow," Todd said, his voice a husky whisper.

My sentiments exactly.

Not quite comfortable under his intense gaze, I shrugged. "Best I could come up with."

"Damn good job," he said with a grin.

"You clean up nicely, too," I teased.

Voices from the cafeteria drifted down the hall, drawing

our attention the task at hand.

"Ready?" he asked.

I nodded.

We turned to walk down the hall together, side-by-side, but not touching.

Just like I'd expected.

CHAPTER 23

The show turned out to be a big success. The crowd was large and steady, with lots of parents, people from the community, and other teachers. The sculpture Todd and I made drew a lot of attention, and each time someone wandered over to see our piece, he was quick to point them to the table where my other work was displayed.

Layla and Luke stopped by halfway through the evening, and came directly to our display.

"Oh my gosh!" Layla said, looking at our sculpture. "That is amazing!"

"Sure is," Luke agreed.

"Thanks," Todd and I said in unison.

Todd went on to describe to Luke the way we'd assembled the pieces, while Layla turned to look at the pieces I'd set up on the table.

"These sketches are gorgeous." She leaned down to get a closer look. "I've seen one of these before, I think."

My mind flashed back to that day at my locker when my sketchpad fell open I was somehow drawn into the sketch. Layla had been there and had noticed my distance.

"I think so," I said. No sense trying to deny it. "At my

locker."

"That's right." She nodded. "She looks so sad."

I had no response. I knew exactly how sad the woman felt, because the same sadness existed in me.

"You asked me that day if I'd ever had déjà vu," Layla went on. "Why?"

I shrugged. What could I say that wouldn't sound insane? "Just a feeling I get sometimes."

I hoped that was generic enough.

"Well, in my experience, déjà vu is more real that most people realize." She looked me straight in the eye. "And when you're ready, you can tell me what you've experienced."

I swallowed hard and smiled at her. I couldn't say anything for fear I'd either cry or spill everything right there in the middle of the school cafeteria.

Todd and Luke still stood at the sculpture, Todd detailing the use of glue and clamps to secure the pieces.

"No judgment here," Layla whispered. "From either of us."

Luke and Layla said their goodbyes and moved around to the other displays, just as a group of ladies I didn't recognize arrived. It was the last hour of the show, and they made the rounds, taking in each display and talking to the student artists. When they reached our station and introduced themselves, nervousness bloomed in full force.

"I'm Mildred Simon," the first lady said, reaching out to shake my hand. "I'm with the Coastal Maine Artists Guild."

I managed, just barely, not to swallow my tongue. These ladies were part of the organization that I hoped would award me much needed scholarship money.

"Nice to meet you, " I replied. "Thank you for coming to our show."

The other ladies introduced themselves as Janice Smith and Marilyn Feltner as they looked over the items on my table.

When they turned to the sculpture on the wall, they were

silent for a moment.

"That's just lovely," Mrs. Simon whispered.

"I'm just the muscle and the custodian," Todd said, continuing to turn attention toward me and my work. "Phoebe is the creative genius."

"Young man, you've been very fortunate to work with Miss Campbell." Miss Smith turned and gave me a sweet smile. "She's a very talented lady."

"She is," Todd said. "And I know."

"I hope you're considering entering our scholarship competition." Mrs. Simon reached in her pocketbook and retrieved a folded brochure. I didn't tell her that I already had one at home. I was too happy that she thought my work was worthy. "We have a number of scholarships available for young art students."

"I'd love to," I replied. "Thank you."

My dad and Todd's mom, who'd both meandered through the displays, each made their way back to our area as the ladies from the Guild left. The crowd was thinning, but a few stragglers remained.

I was just about to say something to Todd about packing everything up when his father stepped into the cafeteria.

And from the scowling look on his face, he hadn't come out of some deep appreciation of art.

Todd looked strikingly like his father. The same brown hair, same cleft in the chin, even the same blue eyes. What a shame that his father's good looks were totally drowned out by his nasty personality.

From across the room I caught Miss Stockton's eye. She'd seen it too and immediately started in our direction, as if she knew intuitively there would be a situation to diffuse.

Todd's Dad looked around, and when he spotted Todd he stalked toward us. I had just enough time to grab Todd's arm and squeeze. He got maybe a second to prepare before his dad barged in.

"What the hell?"

"Haven't they done a fantastic job, Mr. Miller," Miss

Stockton said, breezing into the conversation as if nothing was wrong. "I'm so proud of the hard work and intricate detail these two put into this work."

The expression on Mr. Miller's face could only be described as sneering, as he said, "Like any of this really matters to my son."

The wide sweep of his arm that accompanied his statement made it clear that I was included in the list of things that did not matter.

"Craig!" Todd's mom was clearly mortified.

"Now wait just a minute," my dad said, taking a step toward Mr. Miller.

I was sure there was about to be a physical altercation.

"It does matter," Todd said, his calm, matter-of-fact tone halting his father's tirade.

I stood statue-still, not sure what to do or say. My dad slid in beside me and put his arm around my shoulders. Todd remained on my other side.

"Have you lost your mind?" his dad asked after the momentary shock of Todd's words wore off. A menacing expression played across face. "First you bail on playing basketball out of laziness, then you drop out of weightlifting to take some useless coloring book class?"

Todd didn't respond immediately, so I glanced up at him. Redness flamed on his cheeks and the muscles in his jaw clenched hard.

"I don't think your son has lost his mind," Miss Stockton said quietly. "I think he's just discovering more about himself. And he's been anything but lazy."

"Excuse me," he said, louder than necessary. "I don't think your opinion matters at all."

"Dad, stop this," Todd pleaded.

"How can you just throw away everything you've worked toward for this?"

His finger jabbed in my direction and I felt the stab of it directly in my heart. I blinked as fast as I could, hoping to stave off the tears.

Todd's mom intervened. "He's not throwing anything away, Craig. But you're throwing away your relationship with your son. Please, just leave before you make things even worse."

"I'm not leaving!" he shouted. "It's bad enough I have to confront you here because the two of you are constantly avoiding me!"

"Is it any wonder?" my dad asked, and I almost laughed out loud, grateful for the bit of humor.

Mr. Miller stepped toward my dad, but before he could say anything, Todd got between them. Standing eye-to-eye with his dad, I thought how he looked so much more a man than his father.

"Go home, Dad. Mom and I will follow. You can say whatever you want to me, but not here."

His dad crossed his arms and waited.

Todd turned to us. "Miss Stockton, can you store the sculpture in your room for the weekend?"

"Of course," she said without hesitation.

"Thanks. I'm really sorry about this."

He took a step back and mouthed the words "I'll call you" to me, before turning to follow his parents out the door.

If I needed a reminder that nothing would ever work out between Todd and me that was certainly it.

***

At eleven o'clock I finally looked up from my sketchpad and let my gaze drift around my studio. In two hours, I'd managed to do two sketches of the man and woman I'd seen in the clearing last weekend. The first was of the two of them reaching for each other as their forms faded. The second showed the two of them from behind, hands intertwined. I really had no idea where the inspiration for the drawings had come from. I just knew when I got home from the art show I needed something else to occupy my mind.

That the sketches turned out really nice was an added bonus.

The ugly episode with Todd's dad created such a mix of emotions in me. Anger, hurt, sadness, confusion. I couldn't understand how a father could be so cruel to his own child. And what was with the awful hatred spewed in my direction? He didn't even know me.

I figured I'd never have answers to those questions so I might as well quit thinking about them.

Instead, I opened my laptop and headed to the Otherworldly forum. If anything could take my mind of what had happened tonight, talk of skinwalking curses cast by Druid priestesses might be just the thing.

When I saw the skinwalking thread at the top of the discussion list my heart sped up. It seemed to take forever for the post to load once I clicked to open it.

And as I read the post by *ResearcherGuy*, my pulse hammered even harder.

In my research I read about a book that supposedly exists. The book is said to contain the details of the curse, as well as clues about breaking it. According to my studies, the book looks more like a journal, with soft, brown leather-type binding. The word "Choice" is supposed to be written on the front in some kind of old-style script. I was told if you found the book, you found the answer.

I was still trying to wrap my mind around what I'd read when my phone buzzed against the surface of my desk.

Todd.

"Have you seen the website?" Todd asked as soon as I answered.

"Yes. Just now." I swiveled my chair to double check that my door was closed. Definitely didn't want my dad overhearing this. "Wish we knew where to find that book."

"I've seen it," Todd said, stunning me into silence.

When his words sank in, I nearly dropped the phone as I turned back to my computer to read the description of the book once again.

"Are you serious?"

"A long time ago I used to snoop around in my dad's office at home," he said. "I guess it was some sort of subconscious attempt to get to know him. I was about nine years old when I saw that book. It was in the bottom of one of his desk drawers, underneath a bunch of catalogs with building supplies and that sort of stuff. I had no idea what it was, just that it was interesting looking. I was just about to open it when he came in and caught me."

I shuddered to think how his dad reacted to his snooping, and at the same time I wondered what in the world his dad was doing with the book.

Todd went on. "He was so angry. Angrier than I'd ever seen him. I thought he was going to hit me. He grabbed the book from my hands and yanked me up by the arm and told me to get out and never come back in his office again."

Tears pricked the back of my eyes at the mental image Todd had just painted. "I'm so sorry," I whispered.

"He said, 'You have no idea what you almost did', only he didn't so much as say as he did scream it. We'd never been close and he'd never really been involved in my life, but that was the beginning of the end of our relationship. Tonight was the nail in the coffin."

"I hate that I'm causing such a rift between the two of you," I said.

"Do. Not. Blame. Yourself." Todd's voice was stern, almost harsh. "You are not responsible for this. He is."

And how could I argue with that? "Okay," I said. "Are you alright? I was so worried about you and your mom going home with him."

"I'm fine. He yelled for a while and told me what a mess I was making of my life. I told him it was my life and I'd mess it up or make it better as I saw fit, but basically I just let him get it out of his system."

"How are things now?"

"He stormed out a little while ago. Said he couldn't stand to be in the same house with me," Todd said, and I wondered how it was possible for a father to be so hurtful.

"I told him 'Whatever'. I was just glad he was leaving. Mom is sleeping, finally, and I got online to check the website."

"Your mom okay?"

"I guess. She's mad and sad, and that's a tough combination for me to see. I'm trying to keep things at least sort of calm for her since her lumpectomy is Monday. I don't want her stressed."

"You're a good son, Todd." I meant it from the bottom of my heart.

"I wasn't always," he replied. "But I'm trying to make up for that now."

"Well, you are."

In the silent moment that followed, all sorts of feelings spiraled through me. As strange as these conversations with Todd were, they were also an odd kind of wonderful. Somehow, I didn't feel so alone anymore. And as I thought ahead to graduation, I looked forward to it in the way I suspected everyone else did, rather than seeing it as an escape from the hell Sky Cove Senior High had been for me.

I felt a bit guilty for being grateful for whatever paranormal phenomenon was wreaking havoc on our lives, but I couldn't be sorry that it had brought Todd and me together. It had given me a taste of what it felt like to be accepted, and despite my earlier declarations that I didn't need it, I wouldn't trade that feeling for anything in the world.

"I'm going to get that book," he said.

Thoughts of him going through his dad's office again gave me cold chills.

"Are you sure that's safe?"

"No, but what choice do we have? If he has information that we need, I'm damn well going to take it from him whether he likes it or not. And I'm not a scared nine year old kid anymore."

"Do you have a plan?"

"I'll wait until after Mom's procedure. On Tuesday, Dad's got to go into Portland for a meeting with a big client. He'll be gone most of the day. I'm not coming to school Monday or Tuesday so I can be with Mom, so I'll have a chance to get back in his office."

"He'll probably have it locked up somewhere."

"Then I'll have to bust the lock, won't I?"

CHAPTER 24

Monday was such a weird day.

I packed up the shadowbox display of animals that started all this madness, along with two of the sketches I'd done of the woman from my visions, so that my dad could take them to the post office and ship them off for the scholarship competition. It seemed so strange that these things that represented such mystery might earn me money for college.

I worried about Todd and his mom. And I worried about how his dad might act toward the two of them.

And... I just missed him. Not that I ever spent much time with Todd at school, outside of art class, but just knowing he was not in the building felt strange.

Art was even stranger. I'd grown used to him in the seat beside me. Miss Stockton had assigned each pair a written reflection on our joint projects, to be turned in on Wednesday. While other teams worked together to get theirs written, I sat alone and distracted, staring at the aged, scarred table, and began to sketch.

The pencil in my hand seemed to take on a life of its own, moving with deftness and speed across the paper.

Usually, I loved this kind of creative force – the kind I couldn't stop even if I wanted to – but this time I found it pretty disconcerting.

Before I knew what was happening, I'd sketched the woman again. Long, billowy sleeves hanging from slender arms. Waves of hair cascading past her shoulders. A pendant exactly like Miss Stockton's dangling from her hand. Even without the benefit of facial features, I felt the sadness emanating from her body, knew the pain and loss she'd suffered. My heart constricted from the depths of her grief.

Suddenly my hand moved and I found myself sketching her face. Every detail came into sharp focus. Large eyes, high cheekbones. Full lips and slightly pointed nose. Whisps of eyelashes and shadowy slashes of brows. A smudge here and there with the pad of my finger and her face was complete.

My heart stopped.

My face.

And then I was *there*. Not looking at her on the paper, but standing *with* her... feeling with her... as she looked upon the man I'd seen with her before. There was an eerie familiarity in his eyes, an expression of worry that I'd seen before. In Todd's eyes. And in his father's.

The woman's heart ached, and in my own heart I felt her misery. Love and despair rolled together in an agonizing combination.

"I cannot go against what is expected of me," the man said, his words cold though his eyes spoke of true lament. "Especially not with one whose ways run contrary to everything we hold sacred."

Lightning flashed in her eyes and I felt the corresponding burst in my heart as the pain expanded ten-fold.

Then she spoke. Resignation and grief intertwined in her words.

"You choose to deny my love because of who I am. You allow fear to rule your heart. Then fear you will. In every generation, there will be one who walks in the skin of the creatures of the forest, at the will and the whim of the one I am reborn in. Until you believe what exists in your heart, and allow yourself to love and be loved, this curse will go on."

Just as the woman disappeared in a blinding flash of light, a bolt of electricity slammed into me, snapping me out of the trance I'd been in. All at once, I understood. If not the how, then the why.

She'd loved him. And he'd loved her. But because she was different from him he could not acknowledge her. Could not be with her. He'd forsaken her and their love for the approval of others. For his own pride.

And with her powers, she'd cursed him for it.

My eyes darted left and right, and I realized I'd returned to the classroom. Around me, everything was as it had been. Students worked and chatted. Random student artwork hung on every wall. Light snow fell outside the window. Miss Stockton circulated around the room, clipboard in hand, probably sketching or doodling as she walked.

Not much time had passed, and for that I was glad. I really hoped no one had noticed the daze I'd fallen into.

Closing my sketchbook, I began replaying her words in my mind, searching for any clue that might shed more light on our situation.

One who walks in the skin of the creatures of the forest. Well, that was clear enough. That had to refer to Todd.

Suddenly, the reality of my part in this hit me.

At the will and the whim of the one I am reborn in.

Reborn. As in... reincarnated?

That had to be it. It was the only explanation that made any sense in this crazy scenario. I had this woman's memories. Felt her feelings. She'd appeared to me, shown me glimpses of her life.

I was the Druid priestess.

And Todd was a descendant of the man who spurned her.

The bell rang, shrill and startling, dragging me from my thoughts. Gathering my things, I looked over at Miss Stockton and found her looking at me, staring really, as if she knew something life-altering had just happened.

But how could she know?

Maybe she'd just noticed how distracted I was.

Either way, I had to get out of the classroom and out of the school. I needed space, and some long, quiet moments, if I was even going to begin to process what I'd just learned.

Shoving through the crowd in the hallway, my instinct was to call Todd and inform him. But he was with his mom, and that situation took major precedence. I'd save this for another time when he could afford to think about something besides his mom's health.

He'd call me when he had time. I'd just wait until then.

***

If I thought the day at school had been strange, the afternoon and evening at home alone was even stranger. Time seemed to drag on and on, as if the night would never end. Several times I thought about going to sleep, thinking that if I could just be unconscious at least it would be morning when I woke up. But I was too keyed up to close my eyes.

I'd eaten a sandwich and a cup of fruit salad for dinner, done my homework, watched television, and even straightened up my studio. Several times I'd thought about surfing the internet, but I didn't want to be tempted to look at the Otherworldly forum. And when I glanced at my sketchbook, I immediately shut the idea down, too afraid I'd wind up sucked into another episode.

Looking at the clock, I groaned when I realized it was only nine o'clock. It would be another two hours before my dad got off work. At least once he was home I'd have someone to talk to. And I wouldn't be alone in the house.

I'd just settled onto the couch with the remote, a bag of microwave popcorn, and a can of Soda when my phone buzzed.

Todd.

A flood of relief swept through me, both that I'd finally be able to talk to him and that he could update me on his mom.

I clicked the TV off before answering.

"Todd."

"Sorry I didn't call earlier," he said, and my entire being relaxed at the soft sound of his voice.

"It's okay. Your mom needed you. How is she?"

"She's fine. The procedure didn't take that long, and they gave her something for pain before we left the hospital. Results will be back the end of the week."

"I'm glad she's okay."

He was silent for a moment, long enough that I wondered if the connection had dropped.

"I have the book, Phoebe."

And just like that, my muscles tensed and my heart pounded, threatening to beat out of my chest.

"Already?" My voice was little more than a breathy whisper in the dark of my living room.

"Yeah. Dad hung around until Mom got out of surgery, then headed out of town for work. I broke the lock on his desk drawer."

"Have you read it already?" I asked, wondering how much of what was in the book mirrored what I'd seen in the vision today.

"Yes," he said. "You need to see it. Can I come over?"

"You don't want to leave your mom, do you?"

"My aunt's here," he said. "She drove in early this morning, and she's spending a couple of days. She knows what a shit my dad is and wanted to help out."

"Okay. You can come on over. My dad won't be home for a couple of hours. We can talk without worrying about him overhearing."

"Good. I want to get this book out of the house before Dad gets home and realizes I've taken it. The broken lock's not obvious, but he'll figure it out, I'm sure. I'll be there in ten."

"See you in a few."

"Yeah," he clipped. "Can't wait."

CHAPTER 25

When Todd arrived, we took a few minutes to unload the sculpture from the back of his truck. His aunt had driven his mom home from the hospital, so he'd stopped by school and picked up our project.

I was thankful for the moments of normalcy, knowing the coming conversation would be anything but.

Once the sculpture was tucked away in my studio, we walked silently to the kitchen. I opened the fridge and pulled out two cans of Soda. Grabbing a half-empty bag of pretzels from the counter, I sat down in the chair next to him.

He laid the book on the table. It was old and leather-bound with antiquated lettering on the front, just like the poster on the Otherworldly forum said. Part of me wanted to open and read immediately. Another part of me wished we didn't have to.

Turning my eyes toward Todd, I found him looking at me, blue eyes bright with intensity. He seemed to understand my silence and my reluctance to open the book. Leaning toward me, he pressed his lips against mine, soft and without urgency. I sighed, reveling in the warmth of his mouth on mine, memorizing the sweetness of this moment.

Pulling back, he smiled and slid the book toward me.

"It's pretty hard to understand in spots," he said. "It's been added to by lots of people. Some of the oldest looking writing isn't in English."

I opened the front cover, noting the softness and flexibility that had come from years of wear. Flipping past the first several pages of faded, illegible writing, I landed on a page dated 1782. The writing was large enough and dark enough that I could make out most of it.

The indentured servant of my father could not be my bride, but I loved her still. But 'twas not enough to love her. I had hoped that the words themselves would stop the madness, cause the curse to loose its dreadful grip. But I was wrong. 'Twas not only the words she needed. 'Twas the act as well. And in that, I failed us both.

The pages that followed weren't all dated. It appeared as though notes had been scribbled in much the same way a student would jot comments in the margins of a textbook. The remarks ranged in length from one word to several sentences, but they all carried a message similar to the 1782 entry.

Too much was at stake to risk what I knew would ruin me. She could not understand.

Even though my heart broke, I did what I knew to be right. It was the only way to maintain my position.

I could not give her what she wanted.

I recalled the vision I'd experienced in art class. The words in this book, however sparse, only confirmed what I'd come to suspect. The man loved the Druid priestess, but could not accept her as she was... could not publicly acknowledge his love for her.

And she cursed him for it.

And in each generation, a descendant of the man she had loved had suffered the consequences of that man's decision to abandon the woman and break her heart.

The writings in the book made the solution clear to me. Not only did the man have to love her, he had to *choose* her above all others, and damn the societal repercussions.

"She cursed him because he broke her heart," Todd whispered.

The tiny kitchen seemed suddenly void of air and the yellow tablecloth dull and colorless, as I realized Todd didn't truly understand. Her broken heart wasn't because he didn't love her. It was because he denied her. He was ashamed of her. He chose his pride over her.

"I saw them today," I said after a moment. "In art class. I sketched them."

Walking over to where my backpack sat beside the door, I pulled my sketchpad out and turned to the page.

When I laid the drawing in front of Todd, he noticed at once. "That's you."

"Yes."

"How is that possible?"

"I saw it," I said, sinking back down into my seat. "The original curse. I think she showed me."

"What did she say?" he asked, turning in his chair to face me, taking my hands in his.

"He told her that he couldn't go against what was expected of him, that what she was ran contrary to everything he held sacred. I felt her pain at his words, Todd. I was *there*. I was *in* the vision. A part of her died when he said that."

"Is that when she cursed him?"

I nodded. "She said, 'You choose to deny my love because of who I am. You allow fear to rule your heart. Then fear you will. In every generation, there will be one who walks in the skin of the creatures of the forest, at the will and the whim of the one I am reborn in. Until you believe what exists in your heart, and allow yourself to love and be loved, this curse will go on.' And that was when the vision ended."

"The one I am reborn in?" he questioned. "As in, reincarnation?"

I shrugged. "It's the only possible explanation. I have her memories. Her feelings. Some part of her has been reincarnated in me."

"And I'm the next generation," he whispered. "The man must be one of my ancestors."

"I think so," I said, glad that he understood that much.

"How do we stop this, Pheebs?"

My heart swelled at his use of the nickname he'd given me, but sank at the realization that he still didn't get it.

How did I gently explain it to him without sounding desperate for him to acknowledge me to the rest of the world?

The sound of my dad's car door interrupted the moment. Todd picked up the book and stood up, heading toward my studio.

"I'm leaving this here," he said. "In the drawer with your carvings."

It made sense. We couldn't risk his dad finding it and destroying it.

A second car door, followed by angry voices had both of us running for the front door.

"Damn it," Todd swore under his breath, yanking the door open and stepping out onto the front porch.

His dad stood in the driveway, toe to toe with my dad, and in the light from the porch it was easy to tell he was more than a little pissed off.

"You've caused enough trouble," I heard my dad say. "You're not welcome here."

"You people have poisoned my son!" Mr. Miller yelled. "He's even stolen from me. And it's all her fault!"

When he flung his arm in my direction, Todd was off the porch like lightning.

"Shut up, Dad," he shouted, grabbing his father's attention for the first time. "And get the hell out of here!"

His dad's expression was smug as he watched Todd stalk toward him. "You broke the lock on my filing cabinet and took that book!"

"It was buried under so many old files the only way you'd know it was missing is if you went looking for it," Todd shot back. "Which tells me you you're hiding something from me."

Anger burned on Mr. Miller's face, and through clenched teeth he said, "I knew something like this would happen when you got involved with the town trash."

"You don't talk about my daughter that way!" Dad shoved Mr. Miller, knocking him backward into the front of his truck. My heart lodged in my throat as Todd's dad righted himself and lunged at my father.

Todd jumped in between them and planted his feet, blocking his father like the linebacker he was.

"You leave now or I'll call the cops myself," Todd said, his voice deadly as he stared his father in the face.

My feet felt rooted to the porch as I watched my dad and Todd Miller defend my honor. I knew the situation went much deeper than Mr. Miller's insults, but they still hurt.

And it still made my heart full to see Todd stick up for me.

His father stomped back to his truck, though it was obvious he didn't want to go. He revved the engine more than was necessary as he barreled down the street, and I had a sudden flash of the truck outside my window a few weeks before.

Could it have been him?

"I should go, Phoebe," Todd said, turning back toward me. "I can't let him upset mom."

I nodded, stepping off the porch and joining them on the driveway. "I know. I understand."

"You seem like a good young man," my dad said. "And you're welcome here as long as Phoebe wants you around. But keep your father away from us."

"Dad!" I said, surprised by the fury lacing his voice.

"He's right, Pheebs," Todd said. "And I'll do everything in my power to keep him and his venom away from you." Then he leaned over, pressed a kiss to my forehead, and said, "I'll talk to you tomorrow."

CHAPTER 26

"Finally," Todd said, sliding into the seat next to me in art. "We can talk."

Aside from a few texts during the earlier part of the day, crowded hallways and different schedules kept us from being able to have a conversation about what had happened the night before.

I was actually rather surprised to see him at school, since he'd planned on staying with his mom. But her sister was still there, and his mom had insisted he come on to school. She didn't want him to fall behind.

"How were things when you got home last night?" I asked, halfway scared of what the answer might be.

"Like you'd expect." Todd kept his voice low, as the rest of the class was filing in and taking their seats. "He was pissed. Demanded the book back. I told him to forget it. He at least had sense enough to keep it quiet so mom and Aunt Susan didn't hear."

"What do you think he'll do to get the book back?" I asked.

"I wouldn't put anything past him," Todd replied. "We should probably move it some place less obvious."

"Already done." I leaned closer as Miss Stockton stood from her desk. "It's in a locked cabinet in the attic. I moved it this morning."

The warning bell rang and Miss Stockton opened class. We curbed our conversation in order to finish the written reflection assignment. I figured there wasn't much left to say anyway. Todd still didn't fully grasp the curse and what was required to break it. It would do no good to tell him either. He had to choose me of his own free will, not in an effort to stop the curse.

"I wonder where he found it." I finished the last sentence of our assignment and passed it to him to read over.

He nodded his approval after reading the final paragraph.

"No idea where he got it," Todd said, signing his name at the top of our paper. "And I'm probably not going to ask him."

I put my name next to his just as the ending bell sounded, and we walked together toward Miss Stockton's desk to turn it in.

"Can I talk to the two of you for a moment?" she asked, getting up from her seat and closing the door behind the last of the other students.

Todd looked at me, puzzled, as we waited for her to continue. I thought whatever she had to say probably had something to do with his father and the incident that had happened at the art show.

"First of all, your project was outstanding," she began. "I am so impressed, not only by the vision and detail, but the cooperation it took to complete. This was exactly what I was hoping for when I made this assignment."

"Thank you," Todd and I said in unison. Warm pride spread through me. Miss Stockton's words of praise never failed to build me up. I hope he felt the same sense of accomplishment.

"Second," she went on, pausing to take a deep breath. "Well, why don't we sit down?"

We returned to our table and sat in our usual seats. Miss

Stockton sat across from us, the red pendant I was so fascinated by hanging, as always, from her neck.

"I know what is going on between the two of you." Her words were soft, and for a moment I wondered what she meant. Did she know there was more than collaboration on a school project between Todd and me? And if so, what did it matter to her?

The confusion must've shown on my face, because she quickly continued. "I know about the shifting. The skinwalking."

Todd grabbed my hand and squeezed and I gasped so loudly I thought the office secretary down the hall probably heard me. I wanted to look at Todd but couldn't. I was too stunned by Miss Stockton's words to move. His grip on my hand didn't loosen, so I knew he was feeling the same immense shock.

"You're going to have to give us a bit more of an explanation," Todd said, his voice surprisingly level considering the bomb Miss Stockton had just dropped on us.

And how smart to phrase his response that way, not admitting to anything but making it clear we needed to hear more. His shrewd intelligence was just one more layer I'd discovered that made my love for him grow.

"I know what you're experiencing because it happened to me, too." She leaned closer, propped on her elbows, hands absently fiddling with the pendant. "When I was your age, the same thing happened to me."

"To you?" Todd asked, and I thanked my lucky stars that he seemed to remember how to use his vocal cords, because clearly I had forgotten.

"Well, not only to me," she said, a smile tugging at the corners of her mouth. "I was young and in love with a boy who was totally out of my league, at least as far as the rest of this high school was concerned."

I mentally did the math. Miss Stockton was thirty-five, which meant she was a student here about seventeen years ago. I figured the same social expectations existed then that existed now. I'd never considered it before, but Miss Stockton was probably just like me.

Which meant...

"We discovered the skinwalking quite by accident, much the same way I imagine you two did. Sketching has always been my go-to, the same way carving is yours," she said, gesturing to me. "The first time it happened, the two of us had collided in the front office. I was coming in as he was leaving. He mumbled an apology and I told him it was no big deal. It was the first words we'd spoken to each other. That night, I was sketching an Irish terrier, similar to the one I'd had as a child, when the world around me became fuzzy and in front of me I saw a field."

She'd just described what Todd and I had experienced that first time, everything from running into each other – literally – at Pierce's Hardware to the way my surroundings fell away and I saw the floor of the forest.

"It took a while for us to figure out what was happening. Much more time than it took the two of you. And during that time, we fell in love. It was sweet and urgent, the way first love always is. And it was a secret. Because, as I said, he was completely out of my league."

"How did you stop it?" I whispered. Apparently, I'd rediscovered my voice. I knew what it took to break the curse, but Miss Stockton had never been married, and to my knowledge, she didn't have a boyfriend. Of course, that didn't mean that there wasn't someone somewhere.

"We kept our relationship a secret," she said, not answering my question. "I told myself it was for both our sakes, knowing the ridicule we'd face if our peers knew. But deep down I knew the reason for the secrecy. For as real as his love was for me, he was ashamed of me."

Todd squeezed my hand again and scooted closer until his shoulder touched mine.

"In the end, we couldn't make it work, and he returned to his previous girlfriend behind my back." Her eyes were a million miles away as she continued. "I was heartbroken, of course. I thought the strange connection would be broken once we were apart, but it wasn't."

"What did you do?" Todd asked.

"I left," she replied. "It was the only way. I went to Seattle to live with my father and finished high school there. If I was close to the boy, the one I'd loved, the skinwalking episodes would continue. The connection between us just would not sever." She closed her hands around the pendant, pausing for just a moment. "But I began researching. I knew it was probably futile, but I wanted to know the cause of what we'd experienced. I wanted an explanation."

I thought of the book now locked in my attic and wondered if she'd seen it.

"I traveled a lot," she said. "And studied abroad during college. It was during that time I discovered the curse."

"Where?" I asked, now somehow starving for the answer.

"Scotland," she answered. "I was fascinated by the Druids. So much of their history and tradition is a mystery. I began devouring everything I could find on the subject. The curse wasn't even on my mind then. I was just curious. But I suppose my curiosity was somehow leading me to what I needed to know."

I was mesmerized by the thought of Miss Stockton just randomly happening upon the curse that had caused her so much heartache. It could not have been coincidence. Somehow, something was directing her to the information she needed.

"Through my research I found this amulet," she said, holding up the pendant that so intrigued me. "The agate in the amulet is said to protect against bad dreams, provide strength, and also provide a shield for the wearer. Wearing this pendant keeps the curse from activating. It means I can be here, in close proximity to the man who was the boy I loved, without initiating the skinwalking when I sketch."

"So, he's still here?" Todd asked. "In Sky Cove? Who is he?"

Miss Stockton dropped her eyes and sighed for a

moment. She didn't speak. I thought how much it still must hurt.

When she didn't respond, Todd continued.

"The amulet breaks the curse." He leaned closer, bracing his elbows on the table. "Where can we get one?"

Miss Stockton shook her head. "I wish it was that easy. The amulet only breaks the connection between the two people, but the curse remains in tact. And to my knowledge, this is the only one."

A part of me felt desperately sorry for all that she'd suffered. But another part of me was angry. How could she have kept this from us? Especially once she began to suspect what we were going through. How could she just let all this blindside us when she could've warned us?

"Why didn't you tell us?" I asked. "You should've given us some kind of warning."

"Oh Phoebe," she said, her eyes shining with tears. "I wanted to. So badly. When you drew Todd's name that first day, I knew deep in my heart what was about to happen."

"Then why did you say nothing?" I asked, my voice rising, giving away my feelings of frustration.

"Would you have believed me?" she asked, her words soft and gentle. "If I'd told you all this before you'd experienced it for yourselves, how could you have possibly believed any of it."

"This has been going on for weeks," I said, my tone sharp and heated.

"Pheebs," Todd whispered, squeezing my hand again.

"No." I cut my eyes toward Todd. "We've been going through all sorts of hell since New Years and she's known all this time. And said nothing." I looked back at Miss Stockton, my heart already missing the warm feelings I normally had for her. I didn't want to be pissed at her, but at the moment I could not help it. "Why didn't you help us?"

"I'm trying to help you now."

Suddenly exhausted, I couldn't manage a reply. Instead, I stood up and headed for the door.

"Phoebe, wait," Todd said.

I stopped with my hand on the doorknob, but didn't turn around.

"It's okay," Miss Stockton said. "You have every right to be upset and angry."

"Miss Stockton, how do we break this curse?" Todd asked, desperation lacing his words.

"Oh, Todd," Miss Stockton said, sounding weary and sad. "I can't tell you that. You have to come to the answer on your own, otherwise the curse will never be broken."

"I don't understand," he replied.

And therein was the problem. Miss Stockton knew what needed to happen. *I* knew what needed to happen. But if either one of us told him, we had no chance.

"It's all about choices, Todd," she continued. "And the motivation behind the choices you make. If I tell you what will break the curse, you'll never make the choice for the right reasons. I don't mean to be so cryptic. I wish I could tell you everything. But if the two of you hope to break the curse, I can't."

What a freaking predicament. Would I have to leave town like she did to stop this insanity?

"This has been a lot to take in." Miss Stockton stood and I heard her footsteps start toward the door. "Take a little time and think about everything I've said and all the things you've already learned. Maybe the pieces will start to fall into place."

"Thanks," Todd whispered as he stepped beside me.

Together we left the room and walked in silence down the hall. The empty building echoed the emptiness I felt in my heart. I loved a boy who might not be able to truly love me back. And if he couldn't choose me of his own free will, we'd have to live with this curse – in some form – for the rest of our lives.

CHAPTER 27

"I can't believe she didn't tell us." I flung my backpack into the passenger side of my car and it bounced into the floorboard. "Just let us flounder around, scared to death, and didn't say a word."

"Phoebe, we wouldn't have believed her," Todd said, leaning against now closed passenger door. "At the very least we would've thought she was crazy."

The early February weather was still nasty cold, but at least it wasn't snowing today. I yanked the hood of my parka up anyway in an effort to keep the biting cold off my skin.

"I know," I replied, reason beginning to settle over me. "I just think so much of her that it's hard to imagine her keeping something like this from me."

"I think she's trying to do the right thing." He pulled on a toboggan, then shoved his hands in his coat pockets.

I nodded. Being angry with Miss Stockton was stupid and a completely unproductive use of our energy.

"I think the boy she loved was my father," Todd said, the words sending a wave of shock to the pit of my stomach. Nausea threatened.

Why had that not occurred to me? She was close to the

same age as Mr. Miller. He had the book. He seemed to hate me for no reason.

The overwhelming ramifications nearly suffocated me.

The notion was still bouncing around in my brain when Todd continued.

"Think about it," he said. "The curse said that in every generation one man would walk in the skin of animals. That means this happened to someone in my family before it happened to me. And my dad had the book. And Miss Stockton went to school with my parents. She was a year younger than them."

"But your parents were high school sweethearts weren't they?"

"My mom used to say that. But I know they were on and off a lot during their senior year. The last time they got back together she got pregnant with me."

The more he talked, the more it made sense. His mom getting pregnant would've been enough to make Miss Stockton give up and leave town.

"And Miss Stockton said the boy she loved reunited with his previous girlfriend behind her back," I said.

"The dishonesty certainly sounds like my dad," he said, and I thought how sad it was that a son should have to think such a thing about his father. "She also said the girlfriend was more socially acceptable. My mom was like that. Popular, from the right kind of family, with the right amount of money. Although I hope she was nicer than some of the girls who fall into that category now."

Whatever she'd been back then, she was a kind lady now, and she needed Todd. I pulled my keys from my pocket and walked around to the driver's side of my car.

"How do you think he got the book?" I asked.

Todd shrugged. "Probably the same way we did. Trying to figure out what was happening and how to stop it. Maybe he found it in some family heirloom shit. This must've been happening in my family for a long time."

What a terrible thought.

"You should go home and check on her," I said, filled with a sudden need to be anywhere but here.

He nodded. "She felt pretty good this morning. The pain is wearing off some."

"I'm sure she'll be glad to have you home for a while," I said, opening my door and anticipating the moment I could close myself inside, away from the cold, and soak in the silence and solitude. "Miss Stockton was right. We need to take a little time to think. We need to have clear heads. You can at least put your mind at ease about your mom."

While the words I said were true, my ulterior motive was that I wanted... no *needed*... to be alone. Away from Todd and Miss Stockton and the craziness that had become my life. I need to think, to cry if necessary.

If he suspected my true reason, he didn't say anything. "Okay. We'll talk later, right?"

"Sure," I said, not exactly sure when *later* would be. "Tell your mom hi for me."

I felt a moment of regret when I slid into my seat and closed the door without saying goodbye, but I pulled out of the parking lot without so much as a wave in his direction. I was choking under the weight my own feelings and the truth of all we'd learned.

CHAPTER 28

I stood in the center of the clearing where I'd watched Todd shift, heartbroken and freezing. No phone. No purse. I'd left it all in my car. I just wanted to be alone.

How I ended up here I didn't know. It wasn't like I had fond memories of this place. Well, unless you counted the peek I snuck of Todd's bare butt. That was rather pleasant.

But at this moment, even thoughts of Todd's backside couldn't make me smile.

My instincts had been right in the first place. It wasn't enough to have Todd in secret. To steal romantic moments with him in private. And not only where my heart was concerned. It wasn't enough to break the curse.

The gray, overcast sky filtered through the tree branches, casting shadows across the area. In the shade, the air felt colder than the actual temperature, and I watched each breath leave my body in a foggy mist. The dull shadows and hazy fog suited my mood.

Plopping down on the fallen log where Todd had laid his clothes that night, I allowed myself to finally feel.

I loved Todd. No question. He'd managed to work his way past my defenses and into my heart. I didn't regret it. He was so much more than anyone could possibly realize.

Yet I sat here, alone, tears now swimming in my eyes, because of a curse we might never be able to break.

And that was the hard truth.

I couldn't break this curse on my own. It was up to Todd, and I had no idea if he would be able to. So far, he seemed pretty oblivious.

Agony like I'd never experienced welled up inside me and what had been soft crying turned to wrenching sobs. I couldn't stop them. Love and fear and uncertainty tangled in my heart until I simply could not contain the emotions anymore.

I let the waves of pain crash. What choice did I have? Better to feel it all now, when I was alone, than in front of anyone.

The catharsis seemed to help somewhat, and after a few moments of self-pity, I could think with a bit of objectivity.

I'd leave if I had to, for my own sanity and for his. If he couldn't make the choice that would break the curse and end this madness, I would go as far away as possible... some place my heart could maybe begin to heal.

Using my gloved hands, I wiped the tears from my cheeks, the dampness stinging from the frigid air. I stood up, turning toward the back of the clearing, peering beyond the stand of trees to the rocky ledge overlooking the harbor.

In my mind, I pictured our sculpture, the way the stony hillside framed the left side of the harbor. I'd never look at the piece again without thinking of Todd, of this place. Regardless of what happened between us, he would always be a part of me.

As new tears threatened, I slammed my eyes shut and forced them away. Time to put on the big girl panties and deal with reality.

I took a deep breath, the winter air blasting my lungs, and stepped toward the trees for a better view of the hillside. Perhaps the sweeping view would lift my spirits and clear my head.

Footsteps from behind startled me, pounding against the debris on the ground. Turning around, I saw Todd's father standing in the middle of the clearing, looking winded and angry.

"Mr. Miller," I said, alarm evident in my tone.

What the hell was he doing here? Had he followed me? "I have to put an end to this," he said, eyes boring a hole through me.

"An end to what?" I narrowed my eyes. I knew what he meant, but I wasn't about to tell him that.

He stepped toward me.

One step. Two steps.

And the menace on his face grew worse the closer he got.

"You're ruining my son," he scoffed. "It can't go on."

I'd spent enough time thinking my lowly social status would ruin Todd's reputation. I was finished believing that about myself. And I damn well wasn't going to let his jerk of a father sling insults like that at me.

"The only one ruining Todd is you!" My words rang with force, but I didn't shout. I wasn't exactly sure what state of mind he was in.

"It's not fair," he bellowed. "What you're asking of him. I tried to warn you off, but you wouldn't take the hint."

So it had been him. The pieces clicked into place.

"It was you," I whispered. "At the harbor, outside my house. You were stalking me!"

"I thought if I could scare you away from him, it would save us this nastiness." He crossed the rest of the way and grabbed me by the upper arms. "And I had to be sure. When I saw you kissing outside the school Saturday night, I knew. It was happening all over again."

Fear raced through me. My heart hammered and my knees shook. I'd thought Mr. Miller a cruel man, but at this moment, he was more than that. He was completely unhinged.

But I wouldn't go down without a fight.

"This isn't about Todd at all," I said, trying to jerk my

arms free of him. "It's about you. Your own guilt and misery because you weren't man enough to break the curse when you had the chance."

His gripped slipped, but he recovered before I could move away. His hands tightened on my arms and I knew there would be bruises... or worse.

"So naïve," he sneered, shaking me and causing me to lose my footing. "Thinking this is all about young love and destiny. Some things are just not possible, curse or no curse, and I will not have my son's future destroyed because you want to trap him in this nonsense!"

I righted myself, still locked in the grip of his hands on my shoulders. With each bit of garbage that spewed from his mouth, my resolve grew. Whatever he had planned for me, he was going to hear exactly what I thought before it went down.

"Kirby didn't trap you!" I shouted. "She didn't even try to. She left town so the two of you could on with your life!"

He laughed, the sound of it maniacal. "Only because I refused to play her games. Refused to allow her to drag me into the gutter with her."

I shook my head, knowing what he said about Miss Stockton wasn't true. "You were nothing but spoiled weakling who was too scared to face the truth! You abandoned the girl you loved to save your own sorry reputation and you've been angry and bitter ever since!"

"Foolish bitch!" he screamed, his face now maddeningly close to mine. "This ends now!"

I struggled against him, but he was bigger and stronger as he pulled and shoved me toward the rocky cliff. Time seemed to move in slow motion as I realized with cold dread and absolute certainty what he meant to do.

"But it won't end and you know it," I said, still fighting against his hold "It didn't end when Kirby left town. And it won't end if I die. The curse will return again and again until someone finally breaks it!"

"But the only way to save my son from the hell I've lived

is for you to be gone." He pulled me perilously close to the edge of the rocks, the wind now whipping off the water below.

"You created your own hell," I screamed. "It's your fault! Not mine and not Todd's! You had the book and you knew what you needed to do! You just weren't strong enough!"

He halted at my words, and I saw the anger in his eyes empty into... nothingness.

Somewhere in the distance, a car door slammed. Mr. Miller turned at the noise, looking back over his shoulder toward the clearing. I seized the opportunity and brought my knee up hard into his groin.

He doubled over, his hands slipping from my arms and I leapt away from the cliff.

I took two steps and stumbled, falling to my knees just as Todd barreled through the clearing.

Our eyes connected for half a second, then he shouted over his shoulder, "Miss Stockton, she's here! Call her dad!"

He was here. Somehow, he'd found me.

CHAPTER 29

"Phoebe!" Todd skidded to a stop. He pulled me up and wrapped his arms around me. "Your dad called me when he couldn't get in touch with you. You didn't answer your phone."

"I left it in the car." My voice was a scratchy whisper as I buried my face in his chest. Of course my dad would be concerned. I always texted or called when I got home in the afternoon.

Todd's arms tightened around me, secure and protective. "Don't do that again."

"Craig, no!" Miss Stockton screamed.

Lifting my head, I saw her running through the clearing, tote bag slung across her body, hurrying to get to us.

And half a second later my head exploded in pain.

I couldn't be sure, but I thought the large rock that tumbled to the ground at my feet might have been what Todd's dad slammed into my skull.

The world spun and nausea rolled inside me, but I fought to stay conscious. Someone grabbed my arm. I had no idea who, and I couldn't have resisted anyway. I felt myself being pulled, but I couldn't tell in what direction.

Commotion sounded all around me. Shouting voices. Moving feet. Something warm trickled down my neck. The feeling of helplessness was huge.

A cold blast of wind brought me to my senses and lifted the fog that had engulfed me after the blow to my head. I realized then that the four of us were perilously close to the edge of the cliff.

Mr. Miller had a death grip on my left wrist. Todd's arm was tight around my waist as he pleaded with his father to stop.

"Don't do this, Dad!" he begged, his voice on the edge of sobbing desperation. "Don't hurt her!"

"It's the only way to stop this," his dad said. "For you to live, she has to die."

He'd clearly lost his grip on whatever sanity he might've possessed, and I was the unlucky rope in the tug of war between him and his son.

"No!" Todd screamed, pulling me with wrenching force. "I won't let you do this."

My mind clearer, I used my body weight to lean back into Todd as he pulled. Mr. Miller's fingers cut into the skin on my wrist, but only momentarily. As Todd and I pulled together, I felt his grip begin to slip.

And then we were toppling backwards. Todd took the brunt of the fall and landed on his back, while I fell onto his torso. I moved quickly, sitting up so I could assess the situation.

"Craig!" Miss Stockton yelled, scrambling to the edge of the cliff.

Oh God. Had he fallen?

Todd stood up, leaping over to the edge. I watched as the color drained from his face and his eyes filled with terror.

"Hang on, Dad," he shouted.

Dizziness crept in on me once again, but I managed to crawl closer to the hillside, next to where Miss Stockton stood. When I looked over I saw Mr. Miller hanging on to a thin rock ledge about six feet below the top.

There was no way Todd could reach him.

My heart sank and splintered. How could a son ever recover from something as awful as this?

Todd returned to the edge carrying a stick as big around as my arm. Dangling it over the edge, he urged his father to grab on.

"Can you grab it, Dad?" he yelled.

Mr. Miller flexed his fingers but didn't loosen his tenuous grip on the rocks. If he let go with one hand to try and grab the stick he would surely slip.

"Just try, Dad!" Todd shouted.

Mr. Miller just shook his head, his eyes darting over to me. He didn't even look scared. All that filled his expression was hatred.

For me.

And for Miss Stockton.

How miserable he must've been all these years, denying what he'd felt for her. Yet, I couldn't be completely sorry that he'd done that, for in his betrayal of Miss Stockton, Todd had been conceived. And regardless of the broken heart that probably awaited me, I was immensely glad Todd existed.

"It's too short, Todd," Miss Stockton said, her voice somehow both insistent and calming at the same time. "I can help."

She ran back to the clearing to where she'd thrown her bag earlier. Digging inside, I watched as she retrieved a sketchpad and pencil.

Returning the edge of the cliff in a matter of seconds, she pulled the amulet she was never without up over her head and handed it to me.

My pulse pounded in my head and my heart raced, heating my skin even as the air surrounding me turned from freezing to frigid.

"I'll sketch a bird, Craig," she yelled down at him. "Then you can fly to safety."

If anyone else had heard that statement they'd think she'd

lost her mind. But, having experienced it first hand, I knew it was the only way Todd's dad was going to survive.

"No!" He shook his head vehemently. "I'll never be connected to you like that again!"

Dear God. He'd rather die that let her save him.

"Dad, it's the only way," Todd said. "Let her help you."

"Not while she lives." He nodded toward me with so much fury. I swore I could feel it in the pit of my stomach. "It's your choice, Todd!"

"What?" Todd said, his voice shaky. "You want me to just throw her over the edge?"

"She must die!" he screamed, his voice half-crazed. He didn't even sound like himself anymore.

"You've lost your mind!" Todd barked, scooting over and putting his arms around me. "I'm not going to kill her!"

For a moment they stared, father and son, Todd's honor clashing brutally with his father's insanity.

"Sketch him, Miss Stockton," Todd insisted, his voice a tense whisper. "Now!"

"Your choice, son," Mr. Miller said, his eyes dead and cold as he looked at Todd. "Your choice."

And then he let go.

CHAPTER 30

The nausea that threatened me earlier erupted full force and whatever contents were in my stomach came heaving back. Todd leaned into me, one hand around my waist and the other holding my hair back.

When the retching ended, he held on, gently rocking us back and forth, burying his face in my neck while he cried.

I lifted my hand to where his rested on my stomach, lacing our fingers together in a show of comfort.

The pounding in my head began again, or maybe it hadn't ever stopped. But now that the danger had passed, my skull felt like it might split in two.

My other hand still clutched Miss Stockton's amulet. Glancing over, I saw her wiping tears and pulling her phone from her pocket.

"Your father committed suicide, Todd," she said, soft yet matter-of-fact. "We tried to stop him but he couldn't grasp reality. He told us he just couldn't deal with it all anymore."

Which was, in a nutshell, what had happened. Minus the fact that he tried to kill me and made Todd choose between the two of us.

God, what a mess.

"That's what we're going to tell the police," she said, dialing 911. "We begged and tried to reason with him, but he wouldn't listen to us and fell to his death."

She placed the call to the authorities, then dug around in her bag and found a handkerchief, which she handed to me and said to press against what was most likely a nasty gash in the back of my head.

Todd hadn't said anything. He just sat beside me, still leaned against my side.

"I'm so sorry," I whispered.

He shook his head but didn't look at me. "You're not the one to blame."

"But I still feel terrible."

Bringing his legs up, he propped his elbows on his raised knees and hung his head. I figured he needed the silence, so I didn't say anything else.

As the sirens approached, Miss Stockton sat down next to me. She hugged me against her and checked the wound on my head. Her hands were gentle as she moved my hair from the area behind my ear.

"It's not as bad as I thought," she said. "A few stitches and you should be fine."

I nodded, silent tears escaping my eyes. I still could not believe all that had happened.

Todd's father was dead. And Todd might never be able to look at me again without thinking of the reason his father died.

At least, for Miss Stockton, Mr. Miller's death meant freedom from the curse that had haunted her for so long.

"Thank you for being here," I whispered, handing the amulet back to her.

She shook her head. "You keep it. Wear it if you need to."

I swallowed hard. For all the times I'd admired the pendant, I desperately didn't want to need it. If I wore it, it would be because the curse still existed. And what I wanted more than anything was for Todd to want me. To choose me.

Odds of that happening after what had just occurred were slim to none.

Nodding, I slipped the necklace into the pocket of my coat, just as the paramedics and police officers came through the clearing.

CHAPTER 31

I watched the Super Bowl that Sunday.

Alone.

I hadn't spoken to Todd in person since that day. He'd been at home with his mom the rest of the week, rightfully so, dealing with all that had to be done following his father's death. He'd texted a few times, told me about the funeral arrangements, and stated again that I shouldn't feel guilty.

But I did.

I don't know how anyone could help feeling guilty about being a part of a scenario that lead to someone's death.

My dad was spending Super Bowl Sunday at a buddy's house. He'd offered to stay behind so I wouldn't be by myself, but he'd hovered over me so much that I really needed some solitude.

I felt compelled to watch the game. Todd had told me a few things about football over the course of the last few weeks, and I figured I should at least make an effort. After all, he'd certainly made an effort with our art project.

Settling in on the couch with a Lemon lime soda, my laptop, and a bowl of party mix, I tried to follow along, but ended up enjoying the commercials more than the game.

The cut on my head throbbed slightly, reminding me of that awful day in the clearing. The four stitches would be removed after school tomorrow, which would make putting my hair in its standard ponytail a lot easier.

Logging into Facebook during the fourth quarter of the game, I realized it had been months since I'd posted a status update. Might as well remedy that now.

Long, difficult week. Wrapping up the weekend with the Super Bowl. A new twist for me, but I promised a friend.

I clicked to post. A chat box popped up immediately.

Todd.

A surge of emotion swept through me, warming me in the cool of the wintery night.

Todd: *You're watching the Super Bowl?*

Me: *I told you I would.*

Todd: *I was planning on us watching together.*

Me: *Yeah, well... unforeseen circumstances and all that.*

I wasn't trying to make light of what had happened, but I wanted him to know that I wasn't upset or disappointed that we weren't watching together.

Todd: *I guess, in a way, we're watching together right now.*

I smiled, his words warming my heart.

Me: *Seems so. How are you Todd?*

Todd: *Making it.*

Me: *Your mom?*

I'd imagined that this conversation – our first since his dad's death – would be awkward and tense. Maybe talking online eased the nerves a bit.

Todd: *Mom's still kinda in shock. Dad was screwed up in the head and had been for a while. She knows that. The way he took it out on you and me hurt her a lot. But she's strong.*

Me: *How much did you tell her?*

Todd: *Nothing about the curse. And nothing about Miss Stockton. Just that dad seemed to lose it over me standing up for myself. I told her he told me to choose between you and him.*

Me: *OMG.   How'd   she   take   that?*

Todd: *She said she knew he was cruel but had no idea how much.*

Anyway, she knows enough. I think it's safe to leave out the rest. And I'd be lying if I said the peace and quiet in the house isn't really nice after years of Dad's ranting.

God, what they'd lived through.

Me: *Biopsy results yet?*

This was my greatest fear. That he'd get awful news about his mom while he was still dealing with what happened to his father.

Todd: *Oh yeah. Meant to text you that last night. Negative. No cancer. Fibroid cyst. Not dangerous.*

Relief flooded through me. Whatever happened with this curse business, at least his mom wasn't facing cancer.

Me: *Super glad* ☺

Todd: *Funeral is tomorrow. I'll be back to school Tuesday.*

Me: *Don't rush.*

Todd: *Been out long enough.*

Me: *You all going to be okay financially?*

I'd worried about that, since I'd heard that life insurance policies didn't pay when someone took their own life. I hoped I wasn't overstepping by asking.

Todd: *Yeah. According to Mom, she owns the business now. One of my dad's main guys is going to run it now. So our income won't change much.*

The game clock ticked down to nothing, and since I was unsure what to say to him next, I went with something about the results.

Me: *Well, are you happy about who won?*
Todd: *I was kinda indifferent this year. My team's the Patriots, of course. But I was hoping the other team would win. I sorta like rooting for the underdogs these days.*

My heart sang. That statement said so much about who he was, who he'd become. Without even trying, he'd elevated himself to hero status.

Well, it also helped that he'd opted *not* to toss me over the cliff.

And yet, at the same time my heart swelled with love for him, I reminded myself that I still had no idea where things stood between us.

Needing some perspective, I put the brakes on the conversation.

Me: *I should go. I'm still exhausted from everything and tomorrow's a school day.*

Like he didn't know that.

Todd: *Ok.*

Me: *I hope tomorrow goes as smooth and quickly as it possibly can.*

Todd: *Thanks.*

Me: *Night.*

I logged out before he could respond.

And did what I'd become really good at over the last few days.

I cried.

CHAPTER 32

Tuesday morning over breakfast, my dad dropped a bomb.

"I think we should go to the funeral home."

I'd been about to take a drink of orange juice and it was a good thing I hadn't. I probably would've choked on it.

Not that I hadn't thought about going to the funeral home. I wanted more than anything to be there for Todd, to offer some kind of consolation or comfort. But I had no idea if he'd want me there or if his family would disapprove.

After all, I was kind of at the center of the controversy that had led to his father's death.

Add to that, I imagined the meatheads, Collin and Shane, and the bobbleheads, Erica and Tina, and all the other kids who moved in the appropriate social circles would all be rallying around him, pretending as if they really gave a crap that he was hurting.

Which I was pretty sure they did not.

But nevertheless, there was no way I could push beyond them to get close to Todd, nor did I want to endure their stares and whispers.

"Why Dad?" I asked. "Do you really think they'd want

me there?"

"That boy's father put him in an impossible situation," Dad said, reaching across the table to touch my hand. "And he chose to do the right thing. He cares for you."

"I know." And I did. "But I'm a reminder of what he lost."

"He'll remember what he lost for the rest of his life without any reminders," Dad replied. "You'll remind him of what he gained."

I swallowed hard, pushing back the tears that seemed always at the surface and ready to explode. How my dad could know the exact right thing to say was a mystery.

"Okay," I said.

"I've already arranged to be off work this afternoon. I'll go in after the service. I'll check you out of school before lunch. Miss Stockton's going with us."

"You talked to her?" I asked, puzzled, as I pushed my cereal around in my bowl.

Dad nodded. "She's filled a void in your life these past years. Your mother can't be here for you, but I thought having Miss Stockton with us might help."

I got up from my seat then, went around to his side of the table and put my arms around his neck, still struggling not to cry.

"You're the best father in the world," I whispered. "I love you so much."

"You too, sweetheart." He hugged me back. "You too."

***

I wore my black dress pants and a dark gray sweater, under my hoodie, of course. The black pants would be enough to cause speculation at school. I didn't need people commenting about my sweater, too.

As promised, Dad arrived just before lunch. Miss Stockton walked out with us, and the three of us rode together to the funeral home.

It was packed, naturally. Plenty of people I didn't recognize. Family members and business associates I figured. Todd stood to the side of the chapel area, surrounded by a host of students. The boys looked completely uncomfortable in their shirts and ties, and the girls all looked like they'd gone to the salon for hairdos and manicures.

I just shook my head.

I maneuvered my way behind Dad and Miss Stockton, not really wanting to be seen, already regretting my decision to come here. I was nothing to these people, and to Todd I was just the reason his father was dead.

As more people entered the room, we moved out of the entryway to the small overflow room in the back of the chapel. The beige carpet and rose colored walls were nondescript and ordinary, and I felt better there, out of the way where I could go unnoticed.

I'd learned a long time ago it was better to be invisible than to be noticed.

No sooner had the thought crossed my mind than Todd's eyes met mine. My heart thudded like a bass drum and my kneed trembled as he walked off, mid-conversation, from Shane and Erica. As he headed in our direction, I couldn't decide if I wanted to see him or if I should declare a sudden need to go to the restroom.

In the end, even I'd wanted to, there was no way to escape, so I scooted further behind Dad and waited.

And hoped.

"Miss Stockton," Todd said, finally reaching us. "Mr. Campbell."

There were handshakes, and even a hug from Miss Stockton, which Todd accepted willingly.

Then he stepped around my dad and looked at me.

"Pheebs," he whispered.

I said nothing, emotion clogging my throat. He'd used my nickname. And his eyes were soft.

Hope flared inside me and I forced it away, unwilling to risk it.

He looked beyond me, to the small office in the back. With a tilt of his head, he asked without words for me to follow him there.

I did, of course.

And pretended not to notice that he turned around to make sure no one was watching before closing the door behind us.

He grabbed me as soon as the door shut, wrapping his arms around me and burying his face in my hair. I forgot to be pissed at him for keeping me a secret. It was really hard to be mad when he was squeezing me like he'd never let go.

"I'm so glad to see you," he said, not lifting his head. "I've wanted to come by, but this week's just been insane."

"I know," I said. "Well, I guess I really don't know, but I understand why you've been with your family."

"I've missed you," he breathed, turning his head toward my cheek and pulling up just enough to press his forehead to mine. "A lot."

And then he was kissing me, with a kind of desperation I could've never anticipated. Just like that, hope sprang to life inside me and took root, refusing to let go. Sliding my arms around his waist, I held on for dear life, praying the entire time that somehow, some way, Todd would break the curse and the two of us could be together.

"I have to get back out there," he said, pressing kisses along my jaw. "I don't want to."

"One step at a time," I said. "Get through this, then take the next step."

"I'm not sure what the next step is," he whispered, his mouth finding my ear. "But I don't want to take it alone."

"I'll be here." The words left my mouth and I couldn't make myself regret them. In that moment I knew, it didn't matter what the status of the curse was, I wouldn't leave him.

I thought of Miss Stockton's amulet, now tucked away in my studio, and knew that if it came to it, I would wear the pendant and be Todd's secret.

***

When I got home from the service I changed into my baggy jeans and hoodie and headed for the harbor. I didn't have it in me to brave the cold, so I parked as close as I could and sat in my car, heater running, and stared out at the water.

My sketchbook lay in the passenger seat, but no part of me wanted to pick it up. I felt lost, broken. Inside me, love for Todd grew bigger and more intense every moment. But as my feelings for him increased, so did my fear that he could never truly return them.

Inside the pocket of my sweatshirt, my hand closed around Miss Stockton's amulet. I considered putting it on, but I just couldn't. Not yet.

I was absolutely miserable.

Chapter 33

Wednesday morning Todd returned to school. His presence was met with hugs and lots of pats on the back and more sympathy than it was possible for one high school student body to express.

I got the curious stares. By this time, word had spread that I'd somehow been involved in the incident that preceded Mr. Miller's death. People wondered why I was so entrenched in Todd's life, and I'm sure more than a few of them had concocted conspiracy theories that aimed the finger of responsibility squarely at me.

Which wasn't fair. Even though I did feel responsible. None of the morons who touted their suspicions around had the first idea about the terrible reality Todd and I had lived through.

I kept my distance. He had enough on his plate without having to explain away why the two of us were socializing at school. I mean, why would Todd Miller need to talk to me when he could talk to one of the popular chicks?

Just after lunch, the front office sent word that they needed to see me.

Miss Stockton was there, along with Mrs. Simon from the

Coastal Maine Artists' Guild.

It had been just over a week since I'd sent in my scholarship application, surely not enough time for results to be ready.

"Phoebe," Miss Stockton said. "Let's step into the conference room."

Uncertain, I followed the two women into the conference room, empty except for a small round table and two gray, padded chairs.

"Mrs. Simon wanted to tell you the results in person," Miss Stockton said, a smile playing across her face.

Maybe this was good news after all. And goodness knew, I could use it.

"We had a number of entries in this year's competition," Mrs. Simon began. "And as you know, there are several levels of scholarship awarded. But we were all so impressed with your work, both what you submitted and the things we saw at your school art show, that it didn't take us long to decide that you would be our top recipient."

Shock and pride welled up in me, and I knew the smile the spread across my face had to be huge.

"Thank you so much!" I replied, reaching out to shake Mrs. Simon's hand.

"Phoebe, this scholarship will pay for room and board at the college of your choice," Miss Stockton explained. "Up to a certain amount, of course, but it should be enough to cover those expenses at most universities."

Wow. I was floored.

"The paperwork you'll need to complete is in this folder," Mrs. Simon said, handing me a file full of papers. "Some of it you'll return to us as soon as possible. Other forms will be completed with the help of your college admissions counselor as you're making preparations to begin your studies."

"This really could not have come at a better time," I managed, though my voice was still soft with astonishment. "I can't tell you how much I appreciate this."

"You've earned it young lady," Mrs. Simon said. "And your teacher's recommendation spoke so highly of you."

I looked at Miss Stockton. I hadn't realized there was a teacher recommendation portion. I must've looked puzzled because she quickly explained.

"Members of the guild always contact the teachers of the applicants."

Overcome with gratitude, my voice caught as I said, "Well, thank you both."

Mrs. Simon congratulated me again, before heading to Camden to present some of the other scholarship awards. Alone in the conference room, Miss Stockton put her arm around my shoulders and hugged.

"I knew you'd do well in the competition," she said. "And now, no matter what happens or where you go, you'll have the means to cover your living expenses while you study."

She knew what no one else did. That despite the fact that I desperately wanted to stay near Todd, my future was unclear and the possibility existed that I might have to go far away, the same way she'd had to.

I nodded, too overwhelmed with emotions – both good and not-so-good – to speak out loud.

I followed Miss Stockton out of the room, heading back to class, and ran into Todd as soon as I stepped out the door.

Clearly, he'd overheard the conversation that just took place, because he smiled and said, "Congratulations, Pheebs."

"Thanks."

It was torturous not knowing what to expect from him, whether he would be sweet and charming or aloof and distant.

"I'm proud of you," he added, reaching out to touch my hand, the brush of his skin against mine brief and scorching.

I smiled, my heart warming at his words of praise. This limbo we were in was excruciating, and yet I couldn't stop myself from loving him.

"Thanks again," I said, moving past him. "I've got to get to class."

"Phoebe," he said, stopping me before I got out of the office. "You know that book of mine that you have?" I knew what he meant, of course. He was talking in code because we weren't alone.

"Yes."

"Would it be okay if I came by and got it after school?" he asked. "I need to take a look at it again."

I nodded, turned, and left the office, not sure whether to feel glad or disappointed that he didn't say more.

CHAPTER 34

It had been over two weeks since I'd returned the book to Todd. I'd met him at the door that afternoon, book in hand, so that the exchange could happen as quick as possible. At first he'd looked surprised that I didn't invite him in, and truthfully, if he'd asked, I would've.

But he didn't, seeming okay with this new arrangement between the two of us.

At school not much changed. He was nice to me, but didn't seek me out. He stopped the rumors that I'd somehow been responsible for his dad's death, but made no point to defend me otherwise. He sat next to me in art class, but without the project tying us together, we had no reason for any private time.

He didn't pursue the issue of time together, and neither did I. I refused to make the next move.

We were at an impasse.

So, as I pulled my navy hoodie over my yellow tee shirt that Friday morning, it was a surprise to receive a text from him.

Meet me in the parking lot? 10 minutes before school?

I refused to think about what this could mean, what he

might want. But since we were still in this curse-hell together, I figured it wouldn't do any good to say no.

Okay.

Putting it out of my mind, purposely not speculating on what this might be about, I finished getting dressed, said goodbye to my dad, and headed to school.

***

Ten minutes before school the parking lot was beginning to empty. The last few stragglers who didn't mind being tardy still hung around, but for the most part they kept to themselves.

Todd was already there, leaned up against the driver side door of his truck. The late February temperature had reached forty degrees, which, while not warm, was certainly better than the teens and twenties we enjoyed most of the winter.

His red jacket hung open over his Sky Cover Senior High Football sweatshirt. His hair hadn't been cut in a while, and the ends sort of curled up around his ears and neck. Ridiculous, how a guy could look even cuter with shaggy, unkempt hair.

I parked in my regular spot, two rows over from Todd. I got out of my car, dragging my backpack with me, and turned to head over to where he stood.

He met me halfway, right in the middle of the lane between two parking rows, in plain sight of anyone looking out the front windows of the school.

"I re-read the book," he said. "Several times."

"Yeah?"

I hitched my backpack further on my shoulder, and Todd reached out and took it from me.

"It was enlightening." A smile tugged at the corners of his mouth, and I wondered what was up with his playful attitude.

"Really?"

Well, I was full of sparkling and witty conversation this morning.

"I wanted to ask you something," he said, sliding my backpack to the ground and slipping his jacket off his shoulders.

"Okay. What?"

He grabbed the hem of his sweatshirt and pulled it over his head, the toned muscles of his abdomen showing as the gray thermal shirt underneath lifted.

He pulled the thermal back into place and held the sweatshirt out to me. "Will you wear this? To school? Today?"

And there it was. As simple as that. Just those few words changed everything.

Inside me everything tilted. My heart stopped. Then started again, racing and expanding and filling with something indescribably beautiful.

I needed to say something, to respond, to do something besides stand there mute.

Todd seemed to find my dazed, bewildered expression amusing. He chuckled and stepped closer, grinning the whole time.

"Not exactly the reaction I was hoping for." He reached around and tugged on my ponytail. "Come on, Pheebs. Wear my sweatshirt."

Still speechless, I reached out and took it from him. Holding it up, I turned it around in my hands, exhilaration rushing through me when I read the back.

Miller. 17.

His name and number. For all the world to see.

And he wanted me to wear it.

Part of me wanted to ask him if he realized what he was suggesting, but the look on his face told me he did.

"I want you to wear it," he whispered. "I really, really like who you are."

He framed my face with his hands, his thumbs tracing gentle lines on my cheeks. Tilting my chin up until our eyes met, he lowered his face, brushing his lips across mine, once, twice, until finally sinking in to the kiss.

I forgot the chilly weather as the warmth of his kiss spread through me. Grasping handfuls of his shirt, I pulled myself closer. He wrapped his arms around me, his embrace, strong and sure, telling me he knew exactly what he was doing.

When he ended the kiss, he didn't let go. He pulled back slightly and pressed his forehead against mine. Our noses brushed together and his gaze never left my eyes, the position more intimate that I could've imagined.

"And I really love you," he whispered. "I want everyone to know."

Joy bloomed in my heart, rushing through my veins, and a smile from the depths of my soul spread across my face. Between us light seemed to shimmer, the odd connection that had existed between us somehow breaking, yet being replaced with something even stronger.

"I'll wear it," I said.

Todd beamed, blue eyes sparkling in the cold morning air.

I shrugged out of my coat and reached to pull my own hoodie over my head. Todd helped me out of it, the held his own so I could slide it on. He spun me around so he could see the back, and nodded his approval when I faced him once again.

"Perfect." He grabbed both our coats and my now discarded hoodie.

"You sure?" I asked, leaning down to pick up my backpack.

"Totally," he said without hesitation. He draped his arm across my shoulder and tucked me close to his side, shielding me from the wind that now moved through the air. "Let's head inside."

"Todd?" I said, my voice soft as we made our way toward the school building.

"Yeah?"

"I love you, too." They were, no doubt, the easiest words I'd ever said.

He bent down and kissed the top of my head, not slowing our pace as we walked.

The front door swung open, revealing Lucas and Layla who'd obviously been watching. Layla's smile was brilliant, and she applauded when we stepped inside.

"Todd, my man," Lucas said, slapping him on the back. "Glad you finally got your head on straight."

"Me too," Todd said, leaning down to kiss me again. "Me too."

We made our way through the front lobby, laughing together at the stares and whispers that followed us. Whatever disapproval or scandal we were now the targets of was cause for nothing more than mild amusement.

Before splitting up to head to our first period classes, Todd stopped.

"Let's hit The Pizza Place tonight," he said to Luke, Layla, and me. "Double date."

CHAPTER 35

"Are you sure you want to try this?" I asked, as Todd and I slipped into the art classroom. We'd each managed to get out of our previous class a few minutes early, and since Miss Stockton was on her break, her room was empty.

"I'm sure," he answered.

"But what if..."

"It won't, Pheebs," he said. "The curse is broken. Didn't you feel that out in the parking lot this morning."

"I felt it," I said, grabbing a small block of wood and a v-tool from Miss Stockton's supply counter. "Let's hurry."

It was Todd's idea to try a carving, and I had to admit, I was as curious as he was.

I went to work quickly, removing bits and pieces of wood until the small owl began to come to life. Paying special attention, I carved the eyes, working to make them as lifelike as possible.

I finished just as the bell rang and students began moving in the hallway. I looked at Todd, then at the sculpture. Nothing had happened. Todd hadn't shifted. My vision hadn't clouded and faded until I could only see what Todd saw.

Todd's grin was enormous.

I sat the little owl on Miss Stockton's desk just as she stepped in the door.

"You two are earlier than usual," she said. "I made this for you," I said, excitement lacing my voice. "Just now."

She looked down at the owl, then back up at Todd and me.

"You did it," she whispered. "I'm so proud of you. Both of you."

Tears swam in her eyes, but she blinked them away as the rest of the students made their way into the room.

"Thank you," she said, and I knew she meant much more than gratitude for the small, carved owl.

We took our seats, and Miss Stockton recovered enough to begin her lecture on batik. She cued up an internet video on the subject and dimmed the lights so we could watch.

Todd scooted closer, his arm slung across the back of my chair, his hand squeezing my shoulder. We'd been the scuttlebutt around school all day, but for the most part, people had kept their comments clean. At least the ones we'd heard. I figured Lance had something snide up his sleeve, but maybe he was scared enough after that last fight with Todd that he'd have sense enough not to say it out loud.

Without thinking, I picked up my pencil and started to sketch. Todd leaned closer, watching as my hand moved across the page, the sketch taking shape before our eyes. Somewhere in my mind I knew what I was sketching, but as I sketched, each line surprised and pleased me.

It was our clearing. The limbs of the trees swooping down in a sort of canopy. In the center, the woman stood. My own face stared back at me as her arm stretched out beside her.

My pencil moved to the other side of the paper and before I knew it, the man was standing next to her. But this time when he reached for her, their hands touched. Their fingers entwined.

They'd found each other.

After all these years and countless generations.

The curse was finally broken.

THE END

ABOUT THE AUTHOR

Amy Durham discovered her love of writing in the sixth grade. What began as a love of writing poetry soon turned into stories scribbled into school notebooks. In the eighth grade, her English teacher told her she was good at it and encouraged her to continue to put pen to paper. At that moment, the die was cast, and writing would forever be a part of her life.

As an adult, Amy focuses her efforts on writing Young Adult Fiction... adventure, romance, and life-lessons... woven together as imagination and escape for young readers. Amy holds a firm belief that books are not only entertaining, but have the ability to transform young lives. A book can educate. A book can teach compassion and kindness. A book can spark interest. A book can be a companion. Simply put, books can accompany and guide young readers as they try to navigate their way through the twisted, confusing roads of adolescence.

She lives in Kentucky, where she is a middle school teacher. She and her husband are raising three wild, intelligent, and creative boys, giving her plenty of fodder for the love and adventure she enjoys putting in her stories!

Amy loves to hear from readers. You can contact her at:

amybdurham@gmail.com
www.amydurham.com
twitter.com/Amy_Durham
facebook.com/AuthorAmyDurham

Turn the page for a sneak peak at *Dusk*, coming soon from Amy Durham.

DUSK

The buzz of cheap vodka sang through my body, numbing my stupid reality into complete nothingness. Breakneck speed and three liquored up teenagers probably wasn't the best combination, but none of us cared.

The crowded, city lights of Lexington flickered in the distance behind us, and the sparse lights of Rison, the sleepy Kentucky town where I'd lived my whole life, got closer as Nikki pushed the car way past the speed limit.

"Zoe, don't puke in my car again." Nikki laughed in that slurred, drunken-stupor sort of way, as she turned from the steering wheel to point at me. "If you do you're cleaning it up this time."

Yes, I'd proven myself unable to hold my liquor the last time the three of us had done this. Such a proud moment, for sure. In the front passenger seat, Courtney laughed so hard I thought she'd be the one to hurl.

God, this numbness was bliss. The burn of the alcohol seared away all the crappy parts of my life. Family drama, guilt, uncertainty – all of it – gone. At least that's what I wanted to believe.

It was just after midnight, and the humidity of early

August was no better even in the dark. With the windows down, wind rushed around me as I leaned against the backseat, carrying with it the grassy smell of the country. Watching the vast lengths of horse-farm pasture whiz past, I should've been scared, since the roller-coaster speeds couldn't possibly be safe, but being drunk sort of drowns out rationalities such as fear and precautions.

We hadn't seen a car for several miles.

Until the cop car popped the hill in front of us, and Nikki had to jerk the wheel and swerve out of his lane to avoid hitting him. As the cruiser passed us, Courtney and I turned to look out the back window just in time to see the blue lights come on.

"Shit!" Nikki said. "Hang on!"

My shoulder slammed hard into the back door as Nikki made a split-second right turn onto a side road. Barreling down the winding lane, houses and barns sporadically appeared and disappeared as she sped on. I craned my neck around and saw the police lights nearing the turnoff we'd taken, and without slowing, Nikki switched off her lights, plunging us into blackness. This far from the city, the sky sparkled with bright stars. It would've been pretty... under normal circumstances.

Nikki made the next two curves without trouble, but a hairpin left turn was not so kind. She slammed the brakes and the car fishtailed, throwing me all over the backseat, my other shoulder colliding with the driver-side door. It hurt like a bitch, but I was too busy fighting to keep the ocean of liquor in my stomach from swimming upstream to pay much attention to the pain.

But before I had the chance to grace Nikki's backseat with the contents of my stomach, the fishtailing ended as we plowed into something – a tree, a ditch, a utility pole – and this time my head smashed against the door. Digging my fingers into the leather upholstery, I tried without success to steady myself.

The crunching of crashing metal was deafening as pain

exploded in my head, fireworks went off behind my eyelids, and I slid to the floorboard.

Police sirens sounded in the distance, coming closer. I knew that the approaching cop was not a good thing, but the haze in my head refused to let me remember why. Blinking, I tried to get clear of the mental fog and sit up, but instead just collapsed on the floorboard car again. Nikki and Courtney moaned in the front seat, and Nikki fumbled uselessly with the driver's door. Something inside me said I should get out and run, but why?

The sirens grew louder and louder until I was sure the police car had to be right beside us. Out of nowhere, arms came around me. Strong arms. Warm arms. Curling against him, I gave myself over to the safety and security that enveloped me, close and tender, like an old blanket.

And then it was as if I was floating, flying even. Was I dreaming? Had I left my body? I didn't know, and I didn't care. The breeze kissed my skin with a velvety touch, and the strength of his body radiated into mine. Sleep eased toward me, and I welcomed it with the assurance that I was safe and protected.